IT'S A GOOD CRAIC

IT'S A GOOD CRAIC

Tales From The Racing Yards.

You Couldn't Make This Stuff Up.

This book is dedicated to Granny Davis.

by

B J Morris

Racing people are a strange breed. They are a law unto themselves, borderline feral in some cases. They think different, behave different from the rest of the human population.

They work in an industry which works them into the ground in many cases. This job if you want to call it that, becomes addictive; it gets in your blood and it's hard to break free.

All sorts of people from all over the world and from all sorts of backgrounds work in horse racing. They are not judged by the colour of their skin, religion or anything else apart from can they do THE job and how they treat the horses. It's that simple.

Racing opens up different cultures and gives you a glimpse of how other people live in the world. I've worked with drug addicts, alcoholics, ex-prisoners, Princes, manic depressives, an ex-greyhound race trainer but no one is stigmatised we are all there to do a job and they often turn out to be the nicest, most honest people you will come across. Admittedly there is the odd one that a slap with a cricket bat wouldn't put right, and every time you clap eyes on them you are mentally digging a hole to put them in. But that's life. We racing people just tend to be more open about these things.

I have changed most of the names of people, horses and places as I don't want to cause offence, but these events did happen, although they might not be how some people remember them.

But to each and every one of you I have met through racing, you have entertained me immensely, you became my family, I was mum to a lot of you. I've met, ridden and looked after some amazing horses and I have learnt so much about both horses and human nature.

I THANK YOU.

CONTENTS

1

THE LOVE AFFAIR

I never thought that, when I stuck a double page pull out from a Sunday paper, of the most beautiful horse I had ever seen, on my bedroom wall when I was a kid. That I would end up riding and looking after a lot of his relatives.

The name of that horse was Nijinsky.

Dreams can and do come true.

My love affair with horses started when I was eight years old, I was on holiday staying with relatives who lived in Torbay. My aunt took me to see the carriage horses in Cockington. On the way through Cockington we saw the local riding school on one of it's merry jaunts. My aunt took me in to the stables at the riding school and booked me an hours ride, something she grew to regret. That was it. I was hooked. Over the years, each time I stayed with my aunt in Paignton, I went riding. Eventually I changed riding schools to one at Paignton opposite the zoo. Both riding schools have long gone now.

When I was back in Manchester, at the grand old age of 13, my friend who was equally horse mad and had recently moved from Fairford in Gloucester, was suffering from horse withdrawal. We found a riding stable in Offerton, Stockport. It would take us two buses, one in to Stockport itself and the other bus to take us to Offerton. Then we had a fair old walk to get to the stables themselves. We had our ride in a field full of electricity pylons. We came out of there buzzing, but we didn't care. After our ride we would hang around until it was time for the trek back to the bus stop and our journey home. It took us about five hours, sitting on buses and waiting at bus stops, usually in the pouring rain. We were always cold and wet and loved every minute of it. All our pocket money went on bus fares.

At 18, I moved to Paignton in Torbay. Not long after, I bought my first horse. I didn't have a choice really. This horse box pulled in to a farm yard, where I happened to be. The driver was delivering horses and ponies. When the ramp came down there was a cream coloured foal , all by himself, absolutely terrified. He had been taken from his mum that morning and driven from Dartmoor. He was feral, but I couldn't let him carry on his journey to end up god knows where. I bought him for £80 and called him Ziggy. I've had my own horses ever since that day.

I'm guessing he wasn't even weaned. I hand reared him, as he didn't know what food in a bucket was. I spent hours handling him, I broke him and schooled him myself. He turned out to be a beautiful palomino. He was never sick, lame or sorry and he was the love of my life. Eighteen years later he had colic, his bowel had twisted. I held him as he was put down. It broke my heart, but I had Smartie my thoroughbred to kick on with and get my shit together.

In time I moved to Somerset where I worked in a number of different horse yards. I mainly worked in Hunting in winter and Polo in summer, it worked quite well till I decided that I didn't want to work in Hunting any longer, nothing wrong with it, just didn't want to do it any more. As the Polo season had come to an end I needed a job, I saw an advert in the local paper for work riders in a yard just outside Crewkerne. I phoned up, told them what I had done and was told to be at the yard Monday morning for 9.15am where I rode my first race horse called Tails of Bounty, a lovely dark bay with a white face.

2

SEABOROUGH, DORSET

The first time I walked into Richard Barbers race yard, I just clicked. I clicked with the people, the horses, the atmosphere. I have to say that I had an absolute Ball! The other yards I have worked in over the years... not so.I was lucky enough to work for a brilliant head girl. I came to find out that she was a rare breed. Every new member of staff who walked into that yard was met by her. She introduced herself and told them exactly what was expected of them, their tack and pads were in a neat pile ready for them. She then found a member of staff to help the new person find their first horse and help tack up if need be. She rode near enough every horse that came into the yard, if a horse arrived unbroken then she would do the work. In short, she started them off 'right'. We didn't use 'gadgets', we were taught to ride our horses. Therefore we had happy balanced horses that were in most cases keen to do their job. You will always get the odd one that isn't cut out for racing, but nine times out of ten Tina would find a solution so that every horse enjoyed his job. We got sent out on 'jollies' round the lanes and bridle paths in and around Seaborough. They could turn out to be epic adventures. These 'jollies' kept the horses fresh and interested in their jobs.

The yard mainly trained Point-to-Point horses, there were a few National Hunt horses as well. Nearly everything went hunting, again it kept horses fresh, helped to prevent them going sour. Deb and I were the only part time work riders, so we would be left at the yard on hunt days to put the remainder of the horses who hadn't been exercised first lot and weren't going hunting on the walker or ride them ourselves.

That winter, it rained so much, my race waterproofs were basically useless, so I bought a set of farmers waterproofs. The only problem, well there were two problems; the first one was that they were made for farmers and not a 5'2", eight and a half stone work rider. The second problem was the hood; it was enormous, we are talking parachute size, every day it filled up with water and after every lot as I got off, I got drenched, the water ran down my back. My goggles filled up with water, I couldn't have been any wetter if I had laid down in the river. The gallop washed down the road more than once. I was convinced that I was growing gills. With the gallop out of action we rode round the fields. Fields that were full of sheep and their shit. Back at the yard we washed our horses off and hosed ourselves down.

We had proper riders there, some who have gone on to train in their own right. If someone had an issue with a horse, the matter was addressed and ironed out. The rider would go out on the horse with a senior work rider, and a solution that suited all involved was found. I have never seen that happen in any other yard, the problem is often swept under the carpet and the horse then gets the blame.

One day a couple of Arab race jockeys come in to ride out. We were interested to see what the difference between riding Arabs and our rather large Thoroughbreds was. Hmm; it didn't end well! They were put on the easiest horses we had. Once we hit the field one disappeared into the wide blue yonder crying 'I can't stop!' She was on Rimpton, he was basically our schoolmaster and Carly's darling boy. Clearly these two were not as experienced as they thought. As soon as they got back to the yard, they untacked their horses and left, we didn't see them again.

3

SOME OF THE LADS

We had a quite a few colourful characters, life was never boring. I will always remember Carly's first day. She had rode her little scooter from the other side of Yeovil. Barber's was at Seaborough, Beaminster, just outside Crewkerne heading towards Broadwindsor and Littlewindsor. It was a journey of about fourteen miles. She was petrified. She had never worked in racing before, she hadn't even attended The British Racing School, which is mandatory now, if you don't go there, then you have to go to The Northern Racing College, I presume it's so you have some idea what you are in for when you get to a racing yard. Oh dear, that does makes me laugh! Carly did attend the British Racing School and pass her course. I think she was one of the more worldly wise students there.

The love of her life was Rimpton Boy, a small grey TB, who was pretty good at his job. Lucinda Green came to ride him once, this photo is still Carly's profile photo on her face book page. It broke her heart when he died. Carly was one of the riders that I rode out with regularly, her glasses were a pain in the arse. They were pretty useless, she couldn't see out of them when it rained and she was blind as a bat without them. We devised a way round this.... We would be upsides on the gallop, with me shouting 'left, right, straight, going down the hill'. It worked for us.

One season we had a lad who was dropped off every morning by his mum as he couldn't drive. When he was on a horse he looked just like Dick Dastardly, the character from Whacky Races. I remember he upset RB enormously one morning, that was the only time in four years of working for Richard that I saw him lose his temper. We came across a grass snake in the road one day, I thought I was bad enough with snakes but he took it to a whole new level, his legs shot up his horses' sides, tucked under his chin and stayed there until we got back to the yard.

Many years later I saw him in the Co-op in Lambourn, He looked just the same and still couldn't drive a car, he was working for a new trainer in Lambourn, who had taken over training at Kingsmead. I never knew his real name, he'll always be Dick Dastardly to me.

The Wilson brothers were something else. They were excellent horsemen and real nice lads. Their sense of humour could leave a little to be desired, but I got on with the pair of them well enough. Charlie called me 'mum' and his younger brother Tim, called me 'me old mucker'. Ah well, you can't have it all ways. They would lay in wait in the tack room most mornings after breakfast, just so they could dry hump some poor unsuspecting female who walked through the the door.   They were also sods for chasing you up the gallop, threatening to undo your girth whilst you were sat on your horse. Charlie's party trick was to come upsides me on the gallop and put his horses head on my knee saying 'give him a pat Billie'. I would be listing to whatever side he was on, with a horses head resting on me. When got he fed up with that, he started to pick me up by the scruff of the neck and then, just drop me with a slap, in the middle of my horses back. Great. Really elegant that was!

Charlie's racing career came to an early end, when he broke both his arms in a fall in the Grand National. He is now a very successful trainer, good for him, he deserves it.

Ted came to us after he had fallen off over five times on the same morning with some other trainer. He was a good rider, I dread to think what those horses were like. His entertainment was to rip in to our 'wannabe' jockey, that at the time had no idea what he was doing , but thought that he was as good as the Wilson's and Ted. He paid dearly on a daily basis for that idea.

Ted's favourite trick was to canter up ahead on bridleways, find a low branch preferably on a bend, grab it and wait for the 'wannabe' to come belting round the corner on his horse and then let go of the branch, he would laugh his head off as the 'wannabe' went flying off the back of his horse.

This lad didn't learn. One day he was sent out with Deb and myself, we were on walking exercise and this bell end decided that he was going to take off up a bridle path to our right. We called out to him to stop as there was a huge hole in the middle of the path. What did we know? We waited in the road for the horse to come back to us. He hadn't been gone long when there was a blood curdling scream (him) and a thunder of hooves as the horse came back to us, amazingly the wannabe was still on board, a little white around the gills and rather sheepish. It didn't last long though.

The only horse this lad could actually ride at the time was a chestnut called Drum Battle. He was a really nice horse, ideal for teaching lads how to set off on the gallop. It's not get on and go hell for leather, although sometimes we did when the lads were behind you yelling for blood. I like to think that this nice horse played a part in making the wannabe into a proper jockey, which he did become eventually. He rode round the Grand National, that's no mean feat.

When the girls fell out, they really fell out. It was proper handbags at dawn time. Thankfully it didn't happen very often. It was nearly always over a lad. There was a lad up in Ditcheat, who was playing two of our girls off against each other. One of these girls had saved her wages up for ages to buy herself some nice clothes to go racing in. She, as it turned out was the flavour of the month with this lad and the other girl was out, big time. The other girl was green, as in bright green, gleaming in the dark, green with envy. You get the picture? She got a packet of prawns and put some prawns in the pockets of the other girls best clothes. Of course they were ruined. She would have been better off putting them in the lads pockets.

4

DICK

We had a lovely grey gelding in training, not really your typical racehorse. He was built like an 'old fashioned' TB, not one of the finer types. He was called Caspers Case, brilliant name, well I thought so. He didn't have a lot going for him as a racehorse, he was slow as a boat but my god he tried, all he wanted to do was to please. He was quite simply a nice person. He liked to roll in mud complete with his rider given half a chance, he wasn't fussy. His usual partner was Dick, a lad not long out of racing school. As it was wet, yet again, we were exercising in the fields, we were lucky to have this, a lot of yards don't have fields to go round. We were in Dorset, it's quite hilly there, perfect for training the horses on. Not so perfect if you are sat on a mud loving grey horse. Casper loved coming back down the hills in the fields after cantering up them, the dips were full of water. Heaven, for our Casper, he'd get down and wallow like a hippo, Dick was always having to jump off and then vault back on again, until the day he got truly sick of it. He didn't bother getting off as usual, despite us calling out for him to get off. Dick put his feet either side of the horse on the floor, Casper did his rolling, luckily the horse didn't go over, Casper stood up, had a

18

shake, Dick nearly fell off, but was still on board.

As Casper's legs were not the greatest, part of his exercise some days was to stand in the river for 20-30 minutes or so. I was going with Dick on another pointer that day. A horse not renowned for his genteel disposition, I couldn't pull the damn thing up. I thought I'd be okay as I was only walking and standing in the river. Oh how wrong I was!

I always found Dick entertaining, he was bitchier than most girls but he was very funny, well I thought so, but then my sense of humour can leave a lot to be desired to be honest! These two horses were our last lot. We made our way out of the yard, up the lane, then turned right onto the path that would take us to the field where the river was. We walked across the field and stepped down into the river. It was supposed to be a stream. It rained a lot in the winters in Dorset. Dick parked Casper, it was a bit like watching the QE2 docking in Torquay harbour.

Once settled, the fags came out, the phone came out, he crossed his legs in front him. We were only there a couple of minutes when Dick spotted fishes round Casper's legs. We were in a river, doh! With his twisting this way and that, Casper thought sod this and took off in my direction. Dick's feet disappeared over the back of Casper and I was looking at a mini tsunami created by what looked like Pegasus. My horse took one look and decided to join in, I steered him up on to the bank, still don't know if that was the right thing to do, but it was preferable to being decapitated on the bridge in front of me. Out of the corner of my eye I saw Dick haul his sorry ass out of the river, run across the field shouting.

'I'll get the gate'. On my second tour of the field, Dick shouted out 'why aren't you stopping?' 'Because I can't, you twat!' I did manage to pull up and Dick refused to ride his horse back to the yard, preferring to walk, squelching alongside me. On the plus side, Casper was clean for a change!

As Dick hadn't been out of racing school long, he was keen to try out what he had learnt whilst he had been there. He loved hot clothing his horses, it is one of the best ways to get your horse really clean. Dick did pride himself on having clean horses. One of the horses that was assigned to him smelt like an old dog and he couldn't get rid of the smell. He had a brain wave!!! He bought a packet of soap powder and hot clothed the horse with that. The horse had an allergic reaction, and spent the next week looking like a lobster. Thankfully, Richard didn't see the horse, we kept him hidden. He wouldn't have been best pleased.

Dick was a bit of a social animal, anything going on, he would be in the middle of it. Everyone was included in our social excursions, there was non of the 'I don't like them, so we won't include them' crap that goes on in some yards, if there was a problem it was sorted out. You can't like everyone you work with, but you can be civil. Dick was always first on the mini buses we hired to take us anywhere, he liked to be first off at the other end. Most times, he mainly got elbowed out of the way. Emerging dishevelled and near enough the last one off the bus.

5

SOCIAL NICETIES

Our yard had received an invite to Robert Arch's yard in Sturminster Newton, Dorset. It was their end of season barbecue. Almost all the National Hunt yards had an end of season party, it was the trainers way of thanking their staff for all the hard work they had put in over the winter months. We had never been invited to this yards end of season do before, so we were quite excited. We always got an invite to Paul Nichols' end of season do, as we were his satellite yard. That was always held at The Queens in Ditcheat.

We piled off the minibus at Sturminster, non of us had realised just how far Arch's yard was from our own. It was like the magical mystery tour going through the lanes, very exciting!

There was everything there that we could have wished for. Bar (very important), hog roasts (two of them), disco and the ultimate entertainment....... A bouncy castle!! We were in heaven. On the way over there Tina told Dick that she was going to find him a nice girl. He was mortified, he was still quite shy at this stage. As soon as we got there, off she went on the hunt.

We went to the bar and tried to act civilised. Dick disappeared. It wasn't until we got hungry and went to the hog roasts that we found him. Well I found him, the massive pile of baps started talking to me. I was sworn to secrecy, and taking him food and booze not necessarily in that order. Tina found him a lovely girl, but couldn't find Dick and I didn't let on.

I spent most of the evening with the girls in the bouncy castle. You had to go through a small tunnel to get to the bouncy bit, once inside there was a centre pole holding the whole thing up. Cue the pole dancing contests. We got kicked off it when the centre pole collapsed.

The parties at The Queens were very tame. We tended to stay together and the Ditcheat lot tended to stay together. We got on alright, but I think we just preferred our own company, we could relax around each other. Paul would be entertaining various jockeys at the bar. We, the Barbers lot circled the food like vultures. We couldn't get too drunk as we had to be on our best behaviour. Anyone would think that we couldn't be trusted.

Every time we went out, we never left Barbers sober. It became a ritual to get as much alcohol down our necks before, we arrived to where ever it was we were going. Very often there were some sore heads riding out the following morning and the opportunity to take the mick was never missed.

Tina's wedding was at her family home in Somerset it was a good night. I was designated driver, I had the biggest car. I pulled into Seaborough to pick up the lads and lasses in the early evening, stone me, they were absolutely bladdered. I needed someone to navigate, as we were heading towards the Porlock area and I had no idea where we were going. We got there, eventually, I opened my car door and floored Steve, well he shouldn't have been standing where he was. One of the funniest moments was when Tina ended up rolling around the dance floor and realised that she had ripped her beautiful wedding dress. Her reaction was priceless, she looked stunning up until then. I wondered what her head was like in the morning.

As a yard we would often go out together. One of the lads and one of the girls were forever falling out. The slightest thing would set them off, yelling abuse at each other, it went on and on for ages. On the night in question we were at a sports club somewhere, the girl looked really nice. Before long the slanging match started, then the girl flounced outside for a fag to calm down. The lad followed shortly, we were sat there wondering if one of us should go outside to referee. Then we thought Nah! Let them get on with it. Just as well, for when they walked back through the doors separately I might add, twenty minutes or so later, both of them were covered in mud from the football pitch outside. Seeing as neither of them appeared to be sporting a black eye or any other kind of injury, we assumed that they had kissed and made up and finally got rid of the sexual tension between each other.

But no! Back on the yard they carried on falling out with each other. And there we were thinking that all was rosy again. How wrong we were.

6

LORDS MYSTERY

We did have a few awkward horses, not many, as Richard employed people who could ride. One horse who has stuck in my mind over the years was called Lords Mystery. He was a Mister Lord gelding and quite determined to do things in his way, rather than anyone else's. The first time I saw him, Susan was riding him. We were walking and trotting round the block, which this time entailed going up Seaborough Hill, which is a very steep hill, we also came down this hill at times. It was four miles round the lanes before we got back to the yard. As soon as the road levelled out Mystery started to bronk, he kept this up for the duration of our ride. Poor Susan was knackered from hanging on. The next day one of the lads rode him and took him up the gallop, he was foot perfect.

You know when you have that feeling that a certain horse is coming your way? And I have had a good few of those over the years, some have worked out and some haven't, you can't get on with every horse you come across. I became 'married' to Mystery. To be fair I got on with him really well. He was my type of horse. I loved the way his head would bob around when he was happy. His canter work was easy and covered the ground and his training went swimmingly. Until, the day he decided that he wasn't going to play ball any more. There was no reason for it, he just spat his dummy out and refused point blank to go on the gallop. He was reversed on for a while, then he was dragged on. He reversed through the string at every given opportunity, Mystery and I needed to be at the front, to have any chance at all of going on the gallop. The rest of the string would crowd round to try to stop him going backwards, and I needed Tim right behind me to wallop Mystery at the same time that I hit him. We had a routine that worked for a short while. And then it didn't.

Plan number two: I took him along the road to the top of the gallop, he would go on up there. We would canter down the gallop, pull up before we got to the entrance of the gallop, turn round and canter back up, this worked for a while. On one of these jaunts whilst cantering downhill we met two riders coming up on a bend. They hadn't been told that we were going up and down the gallop. There was an eyes on stalks moment, brakes worked on both sides, disaster was avoided. Just.

After a while everyone was sick of this game, we had tried Mystery in the fields, it started off okay, then he downed tools again. So I was taken off Mystery (hooray!!) and Michelle was put on him, she was thrilled.....not. She was a really good rider, Richard sent Michelle and Dick out into the fields, what happened next could only happen in racing. We were walking down the road after coming off the gallop, we could see from afar what was going to happen. We pulled our horses up in the road to watch.

Richard appeared in the land rover brandishing a bull whip.

Mystery decided to canter in the right direction, with Dick on his horse following on behind. Alls well. They come back down the field, make a nice sweeping turn to encourage the horse. But no, Mystery is going nowhere. The brakes have gone on, he's not moving. Richard has gone. So Michelle and Dick are stranded in the middle of a field, where Mystery has lots of room to duck and dive and reverse, should he actually decide to move. Michelle kicked him on for all she was worth, hit him a good few times too. Didn't make any difference. Dick tried to drag Mystery, he nearly came off the back of his own horse. So he hit Mystery, by this time it was synchronised hitting. The horse was not bothered by all of this, he didn't give a damn. In the meantime, us lot, sat on our horses in the road, were all impressed that Mystery hadn't decided to run backwards. Dick and Michelle looked like they had formulated a plan.

Dick got off and found a branch, he ran after Mystery brandishing the branch, whilst his own horse, that he was leading slammed the brakes on. This attempt to get Mystery to move failed........

Dick then gets back on his horse. Michelle gets off, and starts running with Mystery. Mystery likes this. Mystery starts trotting, then cantering. Michelle vaults back on. Mystery stops. Michelle exits the front door. She wouldn't get back on him and dragged a triumphant Mystery back to the yard, refusing to ever sit on him again.

I got my horse back, no surprise there! Not long after; he was sent in disgrace to a trekking centre in Wales, hopefully, with different scenery he would behave better. It was a shame though, he was a talented horse, he won his races on his jumping, he was able to make up two or three lengths going over a fence. He was stubborn as a mule, but racing wasn't really his game. But if ever there was a Gold Cup for reversing Mystery was your horse.

7

PROFESSIONALISM

Very often the 'quirky' horses are the ones to watch, they have something about them that makes them stand out. Barber's taught me a lot about about riding and horses in general. The standard of riding these days in some race yards is not that good, but they seem to think that they are the dogs bollocks. They wouldn't last a morning at Barber's. We all gave one another help and support, if someone had a problem with a horse, we crowded round it, so that it couldn't deposit it's rider in the road or wherever. A horse usually won't muck around whilst it is surrounded by other horses, but it will be reassured by them. There is very little horse sense in racing these days. Those people that do have it are often ridiculed. If the riders don't trust one another, then how can you expect a horse to trust you? A lot of so-called horse people nowadays, seem to have forgotten that to train a horse requires teamwork between yourself and the horse.

Tina our head girl was a bloody good horsewoman, she trains pointers now and gets good results. The jockeys she uses are well trained. One year we had a horse that was plain bloody minded, so it became her mission to make it a racehorse. I lost count of the amount of times I chased her up the gallop, making as much noise as I could. I retrieved her, and the horse from the garden opposite the bottom of the gallop on a daily basis, with her shouting 'come and get me' and 'don't you leave me', I couldn't leave her there, she made too much noise.

Richard and Tina were very good at their jobs. They had a pretty good idea where their horses would finish in a race. If you hadn't done your job properly with the horse in question, as in; you hadn't got it fit enough, they would be on your back wanting to know why that horse ran shit. Thankfully that never happened to me.

Their horsemanship really stood out to me when we had two runners from our yard run in the 2003 Grand National, they were Torduff Express and Montifault. They set off early Saturday morning from Seaborough, ran their race, Torduff unseated Timmy Murphy, on the second time round the course, Montifault finished 5th. Tina arrived home at midnight with the horses. A long day for all concerned, the next day our two horses were turned out in the field. You wouldn't have known, that these two horses had completed one of the most gruelling races in the racing calendar. They were fit and well. There were quite a few casualties that year, but our boys were unscathed. The other three horses that Paul Nichols sent, didn't get round. It's a game of chance getting round the National in one piece.

8

HELEN

My daughter started her racing career at Barbers. It wasn't really intended, it just happened. She used to come to work with me in the school holidays. Everyone got to know her, they all knew she had her own horse, we would box both our horses over in the afternoon to use the gallop.

On this particular day we were taking the babies out for our last lot. They were three and four year olds just starting their racing careers, so it needs to be done right. Unfortunately we had no lead horse, we were going out on to the roads, the lanes were narrow, we usually met all sorts of traffic, including the occasional stray cow or sheep. Richard came to me and asked if I would mind if Helen would ride our lead horse. Of course she couldn't wait for this. Off she trotted, with Carly being mother hen. I couldn't believe it when she appeared on one of the biggest horses in the yard. Talk about a pea on a drum, her feet didn't come past the saddle flaps. All I could think of was that if she came off that, she would need a parachute to reach land safely. But she looked happy enough and I did trust Carly to look after her.

Off we went, with Helen as squadron leader! I was really proud of her that day for having the guts to ride something completely out of her comfort zone. We set off up Seaborough Hill, all was good. We got to the bendy bit at the top and ground to a halt. Our lead horse decided that he didn't like something in a gateway, Helen was kicking him on but nothing was happening, legs too short and all that. So it was every man for himself, we all survived, laughing at each other. We got Helen's horse back to the front and carried on regardless. That was it, she was hooked. Richard had her riding out quite often after that.

We had a lovely bay horse called Classify, his owner worked all the hours god sent, so she could keep this horse in training. He became Helen's regular partner, they clicked, and he looked after her. When she started riding on the gallop he was the obvious choice to teach her her job. Either Deb or myself were upsides her every lot. She learnt her job well. Unfortunately, Classify broke his shoulder in a fall in a Hunter Chase at Huntingdon and had to be put down.

Helen went on to the British Racing School and worked for some very good trainers both in National Hunt and Flat. She took her licence out and had a couple of rides over hurdles, and on the Flat. Fair play to her. She had the guts to it. She deserved the chance.

9

BACK TO POLO

Barbers was a seasonal job, as it was mainly a Point-to-Point yard, it closed down for the summer. I would be given a date when I left at the end of March, to start back, at the end of the summer. Then I would toddle off to do something different for the summer months. My usual thing was Polo. I was able to have sole charge of my Polo ponies which I loved. I was my own boss for the summer. I got the ponies fit, as they lived in a hilly area, that was easy to achieve. There were quite a few of them. I rode one and led the others, changing who I rode everyday until I got to the point where they all had to be sat on everyday.

There is a boss of the herd, as nearly all the ponies were mares, I worked out who was in charge and away we went. I like mares so they made my job easy. Get them in the right pecking order, they will work with you rather than against you. There was the little Chilean Thoroughbred mare, she was sweet but her poor head was covered in melanoma, we did manage to treat it, and after a time reduce the growths. She was a fast mare and quite good at her job, we got a little creative when it came to having a bridle that suited her. Because of the melanoma I wasn't able to use a Polo head collar. I used an ordinary nylon one when I led her, I didn't always have the control over her that I should have. We would ride and lead over fields, around the woods, all in walk, trot and canter, leading up to four ponies. It got a bit narrow going through gateways and the woods, but so long as everyone stayed in order we were okay. I rode in a plain snaffle bridle and a god awful Polo saddle, the only concession to having so many ponies being exercised at the same time being extra long lead ropes, which were fed through your hands as you went through narrow areas, then gathered back up again, as the paths opened up.

This little Thoroughbred was having a cross day, nothing was right with her, she didn't want to play. We had gone round the fields three times and it was time to hit the woods. What a crap decision that was. I should have taken her back and put her on the walker. The mulish expression on her face said it all. She was fly leaping and throwing her head around, I stopped to check that nothing was rubbing. All was as it should be. The other mares were getting pretty ticked off with her. Into the woods we went with my little fly leaping horror, on the second circuit in there, she launched herself on a bend and got hooked up in a tree by her head collar. There was nothing I could do, but carry on and untangle her on the next circuit. I took her straight home after that and put her on the walker, so that she could think about the error of her ways. Then I carried on with the more amenable mares. When they were turned out after their exercise, they all rounded on the mare to tell her off. I find it fascinating to watch how horses interact with each other in a herd situation, and how that hierarchy continues outside of the field.

We found that if we put the ponies on the lorry in their pecking order they travelled well, put them on out of their usual order and it was handbags at dawn. It was the same with tying them up, they would stand quietly all day long tied up to the lorry, but get the order wrong and it was carnage.

10

MARTOCK, SOMERSET

At the end of one summer I decided much to my cost as it turned out, not to go back to Barbers. I had started riding out for a small trainer in Martock, who was called Simon Burrows. He was one of the nicest, hard working men I have ever come across in racing. He was an ex-jockey and could ride anything. He never expected his staff to do anything he couldn't do. He was a breath of fresh air and I really enjoyed working for him. His claim to fame was coming second to Minnehoma in the 1994 Grand National. That horse was owned by a comedian called Freddie Starr, trained by Martin Pipe, and ridden by Richard Dunwoody. If you watch the race, he had all but won it on his horse Just So, a horse that was owned, bred and trained by H T Cole. He was only beaten by a length and a half. If the horse had won, it would have been brilliant for everyone attached to the small yard, a real achievement, but that's not to take anything away from the winning horse and his connections.

Simon was the only rider I have known who can ride a horse with his head in his hands, in any gait. His head girl had been with him for years, she was good at her job. She knew her horses. As I liked working for Simon, I was going to stay with him, hence not going back to Barber's that winter. He didn't have many horses in training, and the facilities weren't brilliant. We either used the fields owned by the man who owned the yard or we boxed to another trainers gallop in Crewkerne.

In time, Simon found a yard with a house, gallop and a walker in Wellington, Somerset, it made sense for him to go. He could expand his string, and he wouldn't be paying extra rent for a house for his family to live in, plus his wife could help out more on the yard. He asked me to go with him, he offered to pay my diesel to go all the way there everyday. I would have loved to have gone, but I had commitments where I lived, so I didn't go. Jackie his head girl went with him. That decision cost me very dearly.

Instead of going back to Barber's, which I should have done, the man who owned the yard offered me a job as he was going back into training. He had a few horses lined up to come back in. To be honest right from the start it was rubbish. There wasn't a very nice atmosphere, I don't know why, the people I worked with were nice. The horses were easy enough and I got on well with a chestnut mare called Deidre, that was her stable name, I've forgotten her racing name, shame on me! She was a bit of a cow bag, but I don't think she could abide tardiness. She was reasonably easy to ride, everyone else complained that they couldn't hold her. She really wasn't that difficult. She wanted things right, start off right and she was lovely. Well I thought so.

The trainer must have thought that I got on well with this mare, he offered me the chance to ride her in a race. He kindly said that he would stump up for the fees so that I could get my licence, but I really had no interest in riding in a race. I like the prep work, that was always my forte. So the cunning bugger changed tactics and sent me schooling to see if that would change my mind. No it didn't. Deidre was a National Hunt horse, she would have had to carry at least a stone of lead, if I had rode her in a race. That was a big ask of a horse to carry that amount of dead weight for two miles over fences, not hurdles, fences. No thank you. Call me windy I don't care.

11

BITCH TITS

The new trainer owned a few horses of his own which he raced, one of these was a rather a rather opinionated grey mare named after a well known character in a sitcom. She was ridden most days, by a girl who came in to ride out before she went to her day job. She was a good rider but not a work rider. This mare wasn't getting any fitter. I had been told by a couple of people who lived near our yard, that most mornings, the mare refused to go any further than the end of the road with this girl. Instead of coming back to the yard and saying she needed some help, she kept her mouth shut for whatever reason. Whenever I got to ride her, I hated it, she had got used to having her own way and proper threw her toys out of the pram when I rode her. It was nothing for us to buck and bronk all the way along the main road because she was in a paddy. She was a danger to herself and other road users. I told my boss and his head girl backed me up, only for my boss to lose his rag and threaten to sack me because I had dared to criticise this girl. I pointed out that the horse wasn't getting any fitter and it was dangerous to ride in traffic. All he could think of was that she came in for free. I should have said 'sod this' then, but carried on, the head girl said to me afterwards, that I was the only rider there at the time who could ride all the horses, and they needed me.

On a cold frosty morning I was down to ride this damn mare. After the argument, I had refused to ride her or have anything to do with her. I was to ride her round the fields, so, no road work. The head girl and myself set off slipping and sliding down the path to the fields, the ground underfoot was frozen solid. There were only the two of us, she was on Deidre and didn't want to be on her and I was on that bloody grey and I didn't want to be on her. We did talk about swapping, but thought best not if the boss came and checked on us. To be honest the pair of us thought we were in purgatory, the head girl was convinced she was going to disappear in to the distance on Deidre, I was convinced this tramp I was sat on, would me bury me at the earliest opportunity. Both of us were half right.

The warm up trot passed without incident, we were still together. We started cantering, then it started to go a bit Pete Tongue. The head girl was struggling to keep Deidre at an even pace and my horse could just about keep cantering in a straight line, with me wrestling with her all the way, but still, she kept sticking some shapes in. When we came to a corner she ducked and dived, shot off all over the place, bronking and fly leaping, sliding around on the ice. Eventually she unseated me, I was hanging round her neck, the underneath bit. Thank god for martingales, I kept calling out to the head girl, she was gone. I was on my own, my horse finally decided to canter properly, but there was a corner coming up and I could feel her getting ready to perform, I had gone too far to get myself back onboard, so I did the only thing I could do. I got off. What a truly crap idea, I shattered my ankle, and broke my fibula and tibia in three places.

Turns out I was going faster than I thought. I really hated that mare.

My boss decided to run the grey filly not long after I had broken my leg. It came nowhere and broke down. Surprise!

When I was mended I went back to Barber's the following season, but I went down the road with a grey mare on top of me. What is it with grey mares and me? The roads were really slippery at Seaborough. The mares feet just went from underneath her, she came down on top of my leg that had recently healed. Luckily it was okay, but I felt sick. Never felt like that before when I came off, but hey ho!

As I hadn't come round from the anaesthetic for a very long time after my op to pin my leg, it was decided, not by me I might add, to put me on a heart monitor. When you are hooked up to these things they tell you to carry on with your normal day. Well my normal day was to ride racehorses. This monitor sounded an alarm when your heart went above a certain level. Cantering was okay, but if you had to drive a horse on, your heart rate goes up, then the alarm sounded, the only way to get it to shut up was to wave your arms around. I looked like a right dick, trying to pull up whilst waving my arms round. When I took the monitor back, the nurse read the results, then got shitty with me because she couldn't read them properly. She asked what I had been doing, the answer of riding racehorses didn't go down well. She all but threw me out of the Doctors.

I carried on riding till the end of the season, then went to work in a pub. Three years later I got the bug again.

12

LAMBOURN, WEST BERKSHIRE

By this time, my daughter was working in Lambourn, West Berkshire, for a well known ex-National Hunt jockey, he was training Flat horses and was short staffed. She mentioned me to him and I went for an interview. I rode my first 2 year old, I couldn't get over how small she was compared to what I was used to. I came away with a job and set about moving myself, two dogs and two horses up to Lambourn from Somerset. A month later it all fell into place. Well sort of, I had to share a house with some other staff until I could get my own place.

I loved Lambourn, it's a proper racing village. There are more horses than people living there. I suspect that if you were born there and didn't like horses, you would be in a living hell. There are training yards galore for all kinds of equestrianism. It caters to all the codes of racing, eventing, dressage, showjumping, long distance riding, showing, polo, hunting you name it, if it requires a horse it's done there. And the characters, well, anywhere else and they would probably be locked up. One person who used to crack me up was a well known ex-trainer who would get very drunk, drive his car up Maddle Road, where the

Jockey Club Estate have their gallops that most of the yards in Lambourn use. He would then dump his car in the middle of the road, or ditch, or hedge, he wasn't fussy. As I was going out at 4.30 in the morning to do my own horses before work, I often came across his abandoned car, he was never in it, somehow he had managed to find his way home.

From very early in the morning Lambourn comes alive, the only shop open is the paper shop, lads pile in to get their supplies for the morning and stock up if they were going racing, and to get the all important bible, their copy of the Racing Post. For the yards further away from the village they do a paper delivery in a car. At lunchtime, the place is busy with lads getting their lunches, before they go home to sleep for the afternoon. The butchers shop not only sells meat, but really good cooked food, they do a roaring trade. Their chicken and chips are some of the best I have tasted, and Lambourn has the best tack shop. They cater to all tastes and can make practically anything you ask them to. It's heaven to someone like me!

As I started work at 5.45am, I got up at 4.20am to do my own horse before work. I had to be sat on my first horse by 6am, and be in the indoor ride not long after. I felt that I was living in a twilight world, I was on to my second horse before it became daylight. Riding in the dark was something else. I found out that there was dark, and there was dark, pitch black, where there was no moon or it was cloudy. Some mornings all you could see were the lights in the barns and stables that were dotted around in the inky blackness.

After we had warmed up our horses in the ride, walking and trotting. We would then go out on to the gallop, we followed the yard car which was upsides us with the headlights showing the way. Reg, the head lad didn't ride out, he drove the yard car from yard to yard. We had six yards spread out over a distance in Upper Lambourn. If he was riding, there would be no way he could get us from the bottom yard safely in the dark, up to the main yard where the indoor ride was. Often riders from other yards would tag on to us, whilst Reg sat behind lighting the way. Some of our riders didn't have cars, he would throw their tack and them in the car, and take them to where they were supposed to be. This usually worked well, until it was our work days on Tuesdays and Fridays, then it could all go to pot. The boss often changed the work board, then he wouldn't tell anyone that he had changed the board, then, he would shout at the poor rider, sat on the wrong horse, as they came in to the ride.

As only the select few rode work on Tuesday and Friday, the rest of us had our car gallop. We swapped our horse for the back of the car, whilst a jockey rode our horse, then we swapped back at the end of the gallop. It was interesting listening to how the trainer timed his horses over a distance and what he was looking for. It gives you a different view point being upsides a horse doing a piece of work. Some of the lads were a bit miffed at sitting in the car instead of riding their horses. Personally I didn't care, I enjoyed seeing how the horses worked from the car. The head lad would be in the car, the boss and him would discuss how well or how bad a horse was travelling. Was the horse covering the ground, did it look sound, was he breathing properly or struggling to take breath. Some horses throats can close up when they start to run, that's not ideal. They can swallow their tongues. A horses lungs are enormous, they need to fill up with air, in order to be able to do their job, they are like huge bellows. Some horses make roaring noises which can hinder a racehorse. It can be a sign that the horse isn't fit.

This is why at the end of exercise you are questioned over each horse. The trainer needs feed back. It's no good telling him what he wants to hear, you have to tell him the truth, that's the only way the horse will improve. On work days the trainer gets to see first hand how things are progressing.

13

EARLY MORNINGS

Going out on to the gallop in the pitch black for the first few times was weird. We were stepping out from bright, florescent lit areas with a radio blaring, into near enough total blackness. The car was there waiting for us to light the way, what always struck me was how quiet it would be. We chatted away to each other. The only other sounds, were the horses hooves on the walkway, the jingling of tack and the occasional snorts from the horses. Any noise sounded dead. Like a blanket had been thrown over us. It's a strange thing to say, but it was incredibly peaceful. The lull before the storm. Getting closer to the gallop, we would pull our jerks up, check our girths for the last time, before setting off. The car had left us to be put in position at the beginning of the gallop. Reg had already checked the gallop, to make as sure as he could, that there were no foreign objects on the gallop that had arrived overnight. Dead animals were the main culprits.

We got in order and set off. Often the horses in front of you had sparks coming from their shoes. We carried on our conversations to one another as we cantered, but were frequently interrupted by the car alongside us hitting a bump or going in to a dip, with the headlights either shooting up into the dark sky or hitting the deck, then our horses would spook, and the language got industrial! We had to put our trust in our mounts, horses can see better in the dark than we can. I don't know about anyone else, but my senses were more acute riding in the dark. It's a little unnerving when you aren't sure of your surroundings, you are on a strange horse and you can't see jack shit. The colts are always at the front and the fillies are at the back, you hope that no one comes off a colt, especially in the dark. You can be ran off with, but don't come off.

14

RAG DOLL

In my first week, I grew accustomed to having my car hi-jacked with anything from four to six riders and their tack. They would all pile in to my car, to get to the various yards that our boss had scattered around. It was a good thing that it was an estate. At our yard we didn't muck out in the morning, we had quite a few lots to get through, it was nothing to have five or six lots a day. The usual was, three lots before breakfast at nine. We did evening stables as usual, but we had five-six horses each to muck out, hay, water, brush and rug up.

One of my horses was a three year old chestnut colt, he had problems with his legs. Then to add insult to injury, he had a wind op. He had been on box rest for ages, I think it's fair to say that he had lost the plot. The first time I opened his door he scared the living shit out of me. He launched himself from the back of his stable to the door in one leap, standing over me on his back legs. He was like a giant puppy, he wanted to play, but had no idea of his size or even spacial awareness. Eventually, I managed to get in the stable, get his head collar on, I barely made it to the back of the stable to put him on his chain, I was like a rag doll on a bit of rope. Then I found the easy part, he loved to be fussed over. I was convinced that I was going to be posted out of the stable at great speed when I did his feet, but no, he was a perfect gentleman. When I let him down, he was jumping about all over the place. We got to the door in a heap, with me hanging on for grim death, rag doll moment again. Somehow I got the head collar off and shut the door quickly, as his head shot out through the anti-weave grill.

From then on, I resolved to have mints on me and teach him not to terrorise me. He was a sweet horse, but so stressed at never coming out of his box. The horse in the box next to him was another colt on box rest. A beautiful dark bay, with a white blaze, this horse was stunning, his sire was Sadlers Wells, he was the dead spit of his dad. He, hadn't lost the plot. When he started to be ridden again he was sold, and the new owner wanted him gelded. That horse was never the same again and I don't mean because a couple of dangly bits were missing. His coat was dull, he lost condition, he looked awful, he was a shadow of his former self. Such a shame.

This yard was also a dealing yard for racehorses, not just a training yard. We had a high turn over of horses, they were forever being moved around, and we the staff, were moved around between the six yards on evening stables. We rarely got the same horses week in, week out. But you learnt to handle anything and everything. Some you got on with and some you didn't.

15

EDUCATION

My first week was certainly an education. I got sent off with some of the other lads, in a couple of lorries to pick up twelve horses from a stud down the M4. We were to get the five fillies first, when we pulled up to their field they eyed us with great suspicion. Thankfully, they all still had their head collars on with their name tags still attached. I couldn't believe their names, they were named after The Twelve days of Christmas. All, but one loaded nicely, she was determined not to go home. We got her on the lorry eventually, after a right royal tantrum from one of the lads who happened to be Pakistani. The language! All in perfect English. He got such a telling off from one of the lorry drivers, that he sulked for the rest of the day. With the fillies loaded up, we drove on to the colts field, they were ready to come home, they were also named after The Twelve Days of Christmas, so we had the full deck!

My boss' children had named these horses, when he was stuck with naming something he asked his children for ideas. He had one dark grey colt that was named Clippity Clop, it was by Clodivil. It was well named, I rode it frequently, I didn't get on with it. That was the only one I fell off whilst I was there. I got bucked off in the ride one freezing cold morning. A horse tends to put his ears back when he is going to buck, the bigger the horse, the bigger the telegram that he is going to do something. Not Clippity. His ears would be forward as he did his handstands, they couldn't be described any other way. He wasn't particularly big but there was never any warning about what he was going to do.

Often, my last lot of the day would be to ride my boss' hunter, I could do whatever I wanted with him, I went on jollies all over the place. When I was asked to take his children with me, all his daughter wanted to do was to ride on the gallop, as fast as she could. Her pony was like shit off a shovel, her little legs would be flapping like anything, yelling over her shoulder.
'Faster Billie, faster'. Her brother didn't really want to ride, he was a little scared of the whole idea of going 'faster'.

Fast forward a few years, his daughter has been on the British Junior Eventing team and now rides out for her father. She has taken her licence out to ride on the flat.

16

YEARLINGS

Being a flat yard we trained yearlings. Once they had been lunged, long reined and backed, we, the riders, got on them. I had never sat on a yearling before I came to Lambourn, the lady who broke them in was good at her job. It's a case of transferring what the horse had been taught on the ground, as in, go, stop, turn left or right, to interpreting these instructions from a rider on his back. I had also never sat on a horse that was 'juiced up', it's quite a common thing to dope a horse if you think it's going to be a problem. Personally I don't like it, I never felt safe riding something that was falling over it's own feet. But it's something that is done on a regular basis with fresh horses, the idea behind it is to minimise accidents to both horse and rider.

The first day we rode our yearlings they had a little bit of dope in them. They were only doped for a couple of days, hopefully, they were getting the idea of what was expected of them. We all trooped in to the ride for walking and trotting. That was horrible, all legs and unbalanced babies. After a couple of weeks of going round in circles in the ride we progressed to canter, it wasn't as bad as it could have been, everyone stayed on. Not long after that, when the canter work was established in the ride, our boss appeared, announcing that we were going out on to the gallop for the first time. Can't wait.

We had the bravest colt at the front. We had no lead horse, we were it. We had to go through a chicane, which took us in to a field that we had to ride across, to reach the gallop on the other side, that we were going to be using. Well, these little horses had never had to twist their bodies to get through railings before and certainly not with a rider on board. This unsettled them. There were also some horses using the other gallop. Our horses were on sensory overload, waiting for the blue touch paper to be lit. Once we were all through the chicane, the call went out 'trot on'. The colt at the front snorted, then it was like a Mexican wave going down the string. One minute all ten youngsters were together, the next it was like a dandelion had been blown on. We shot off in ten different directions, bucking, rearing, farting, snorting, fly leaping and bronking. It was chaos. Someone shouted 'regroup', we got together and proceeded to trot across the field to the other side. We had to go through another chicane to come out on to the gallop.

By this stage our youngsters were tired, we were only going a few furlongs to see how they coped. We set off in a group, the bloody thing I was sat on decided that he wasn't tired after a furlong, and that he would quite like to bring down the horse diagonally in front of me on the right. He kept shooting forward sticking his right foreleg out, trying to catch the colts hind legs. It was a nightmare. When we pulled off the gallop, my colt was still making a bee line for the same colt.

We worked out that the guy who was riding the colt in front of me, was wearing a certain aftershave and it was turning my colt on. This is why, when you are handling colts and stallions you never wear perfume or strong smelling toiletries. It doesn't take much for them to lock on and it's very hard to unlock them. Forgive the pun. Apart from my randy colt I enjoyed riding yearlings and two year olds. You are starting with a fresh canvas. They are weak, but it's surprising how quickly they change. One minute they are a baby, the next you are looking at a proper horse. Compared with riding a newly broken three or four year old, who are obviously that much older, know their own minds and they are certainly stronger. I prefer the babies.

17

THE DRIVER

I became travelling head lass when my boss found out I could drive a lorry. I went on to take my HGV a couple of years later. From then on, it was ride four or five horses out in the morning, then go driving. We didn't have a lot of runners, I found out that when you became travelling lass, you were also expected to drive the boss all over the place when you weren't racing.

There was this one time we had a runner at Windsor, I didn't take the horse, I took the boss in his car. Even before I had parked the car in the car park, he had grabbed his jacket from the back, it had been on the floor and he hot footed it to the bar. The lads had been in the car on work day and basically they had wiped their feet on his jacket. It was a blue suit, he put the jacket on as he walked, well ran, towards the racecourse, there were all these dusty, muddy footprints all over the back of it. A truly marvellous impression. The stewards were clearly used to him, everyone greeted him by his first name, smiled and shook their heads. I ran after him, got to the parade ring there was no sign of him. As I looked round thinking he couldn't have gone far, he had a horse to saddle in the next race, lo and behold there he was in the bar with four bucks fizz's lined up. I watched in amazement as he threw them down his neck, one after the other, then came marching out to saddle his horse. It didn't come anywhere.

Later on I was waiting for my boss to come out of the pub, he was meeting up with someone for dinner and drinks. I had been up since 4.20am, rode out five horses, then drove him down the M4 to the racecourse. 10 pm came, no sign of him. 10.30 pm, no sign. I decided to move the Discovery to the other side of the pond, that for some obscure reason was in the middle of the car park. I parked under the trees, opposite where I had first been parked.

He must have been keeping tabs on me, because the curtains on one of the pub windows flew open and he was peering out looking for the Discovery. When he found it, he went back to his friend. Another fifteen minutes went by, there was no sign of leaving the pub. I moved the car again, out of spite this time, I have to admit. Again the curtains flew open, how I wished he would fly out of the pub that quick. I needed food and sleep. I was about to move the car again, when he was thrown out of the pub well after closing time. Our journey home was in silence with him sulking. With his feet on the dashboard. I had the last laugh. His car had memory seats, as I got out at home, the seat moved right out of the way. My boss was going to drive the half mile back to his home. I looked back as I opened the front door, to see him concertinaed up against the windscreen. That image has stayed with me all these years.

Riding out next morning one of the girls asked how I got on, when I told her, she wasn't surprised. She was asked to drive him in to London one evening to meet some people. The night dragged on and she had to keep moving the car around. In the end she drove the car onto the pavement right outside the restaurant he was in and glared at him, until he came out. If we didn't have to start work so early it wouldn't have been a problem, something he failed to grasp.

The boss found a prospective buyer who was interested in a couple of horses. So off we went on a road trip to Bath. When we got there, we pulled into a driveway of a rather smart house complete with a purple tennis court. The property was quite high up and looked down on to Bath itself. After the pow wow in the house, everyone came out, I was still in the car, waiting.... Always waiting. My boss got in our car, we were to follow the other cars, because everyone was going for a meal in Bath. When we had found somewhere to park, my boss was told that I had to go too. So off I trundled behind my boss to meet his prospective buyer. He was a successful business man 'and the rest I thought'. But he was okay, I got on with him like a house on fire, he had his 'nephews' with him. They looked more like bouncers. We had a lovely meal paid for by this man, but he bought no horses.

A few weeks later he arrived with his entourage in Lambourn. The head lad came looking for me, I was riding out at the time. I had to get down to the bottom yard as quick as possible, this man had turned up and my boss thought he had a better chance selling some horses if I was there. I was to show the horses that might interest this man. Everything that was to be shown, wasn't that great to be honest. My boss stood at one end of the yard and the buyer moved to the other end. Every time I went past with a horse he asked was it any good. I wasn't going to lie.

Under my breath I said 'no, maybe, could be'. There was something about this man that told me that if you tried to pull a fast one with him, there would be repercussions. Best to be honest. He didn't buy any horses.

18

TRAVELLING LASS

Race days could be testing. A lot depended on who went with me. All race travelling people want, are good reliable lads with them, who can be trusted to do their horses to the best of their ability. In theory this works well. Then there was my yard.

I got my piece of paper from the office with my instructions. The key to the racing tack room, and the lorry keys. The piece of paper had the name of the horse that was running, which race course we were going to, what race it was running in, the owners colours and what specifics it ran in. As in; did the horse have to have his tongue tied, if so, I needed a pair of tights, well just one leg, it was softer than the bought tongue ties. Did the horse run in blinkers or visor, there is a difference. With blinkers the horse can not see behind him, with visors, there is limited vision behind the horse. What other head gear, if any, did the horse run in, all this was stated on the entry to the race. If you turn up to the racecourse without the equipment that your horse is declared to run in, then your horse can't run, unless you borrow some from another trainer.

There is usually a list of horses names with their owners

colours, and what they run in, hanging in the racing tack room. There is also a list of the racecourses that the yards horses run at, they are listed from the nearest, to the furthest away, with the mileage next to the name of the racecourse and how long it takes to get there. The best tack is kept in there, the bridles all have their bits stitched to the cheek pieces and reins. You can see the colour of the breast plates, they are not covered in sweat, gallop or mud. The smartest rugs are in there. There are no holey sweat sheets unless they are meant to be holey. The chamois for securing the jockeys saddles are in one piece, not in tatters. This is a hallowed place. It remains locked to the lesser mortals on the yard. So when I was sent racing with a certain yard man, who would argue till he was blue in the face that I had the wrong horse, and I was going to the wrong racecourse, I used to get a bit testy. Throw in the horse having been moved to a different yard the day before, it could take a while driving from yard to yard, searching the boxes, till I found my horse. We had stabling for a hundred horses. Arghh!

With the right horse on board the lorry, all the correct gear, clay for the legs, brown paper already cut, ready to be put on top of the clay and bandages to put on over all that. All this would be triple checked. We would set off, only for him to announce, that we were to pick his missus up on the way to the village. This would be their day out. I had no problem with that. I did have a problem with the chain smoking and the disappearing act when we reached the racecourse. Somehow we would muddle through the day, with him doing as little, as humanly possible, I'm surprised he managed to breathe for himself, but that's going off track. We would return to Lambourn, with me vowing to never go with him again. Till next time. Thank god we didn't have many runners.

Taking one of the Polish guys was a much nicer experience. He knew his job, and appreciated being away from the yard and the extra money he would earn. The only problem was the spitting. It was continuous, although he didn't spit in the lorry, he spat out of the window. When we stopped anywhere, you name it, he spat there. I remember the first time we went to Goodwood, we drove through the golf course to get to the stables, there were people playing, I swear he spat at near enough everyone, I couldn't drive quick enough to get past these poor people. The lorry had electric windows, but I couldn't lock his from my side. I was really glad I had him with me that day as the partition in the lorry fell apart. We had a big chestnut colt on board, and if it hadn't been for the Polish guy with his supply of baler twine, the colt would have been going back home in another lorry.

19

GOODWOOD

Glorious Goodwood. There is nothing glorious about that place, when you take a horse racing. I found it a complete ball ache. The drive across the golf course is cringe worthy enough, waiting for an errant golf ball to hit your lorry or worse, break a window with your precious cargo on board. For the size of the place, the stabling, the car parks for the lorries at both the stables and the race course don't quite go together. The parking areas are tiny. Don't get me wrong, the stabling is good. Back in the day, they used to hold prestige dressage competitions on the lawns, so the stabling had to be of a good standard.

Parking could be a problem if there was a full racecard. We would unload at the bottom of the drive to the stables, then depending on the time when the horse ran, I would either park up in the car park or drive to the race course itself, which was about a mile away, and declare our runner to the stewards in the weighing room. The car park at the race course was a shambles, it was so small. There was no hanging around, horses were either arriving for their race, or horses were being picked up after their race to go back to the stables. Sometimes the lads would check their horse and carry on homeward bound. You were on a one way system from the stables to the course and back again. It was all round China to get back to the stables. In fairness there was a bus laid on from the stables, for the lads to declare their runners, but if you were running a little late it was quicker to drive over. For the lads whose horses went with transport, they would have to use the bus or sweet talk their driver into taking them over, or cadge a lift with some other driver.

As your race drew near you would load up your horse and equipment, trek over to the course, hoping that we would be able to park, often a horse was unloaded in the middle of the car park and then the lorry moved out of the way. Pronto. The pre-parade ring is something else. Half of it is under dense trees, as you are walking round with your horse, you are continually going from light to dark and you are on quite a steep hill. Once the horse was being walked round, I would try to find a fairly level stall to put our bags in, hoping that by the time I had come back from the weighing room with the jockeys saddle we still had it, this was not always the case. Once the horse was saddled and we were allowed to go in the parade ring, things settled down a bit.

It is a beautiful place for race goers, the flowers are stunning. On the big race days, we would battle our way through the stretch limos to get to the course, and to get back out again. The stewards would keep an eye open for the horse boxes trying to get in and out. It's a big ask of a horse to keep being put on a lorry, and taken off again, especially when it was hot. When the horse has been washed down after his race, got his breath back and he's not too tired, we would often go straight home. Sometimes we went back to the stables, it all depended on the horse.

On one of the occasions that my boss decided to attend, when one of his horses ran, he preferred to watch the race on the TV in his office. He over girthed a little filly that was running. She was one I regularly rode at home, as he went up yet another hole she nearly fell on the floor. He turned to me and said 'does she always do this when you saddle her?' I replied 'no'. She ran a crap race and she was never the same again. She was sound at walk and trot, but couldn't canter. I kept asking for her to be put on the physios list. Even though my boss saw how bad she was going up the gallop, all he would say was hit her. I would pull her up, she was not right. Sod that. This was when my interest in equine massage started, this filly could be put right, all I was asking for was her to seen by the physio.

20

CULTURES

I had never worked with so many different people, from different corners of the world, till I went to Lambourn. It's a real eye opener how people live and their different ways of doing things. In India and Pakistan, when they groom their horses, they have to leave a pile of dirt from their horses brushes outside the horses stable. If it isn't considered a big enough pile, they have to start again. They always send money home to support their families. With all the atrocities that are happening in our world these people are just as sickened as we are.

There was the Czech, who was an ex soldier, who would stand up on his horse and pretend that he was shooting the crows on the gallop. We were inundated with them. Our boss would go out to shoot them, the only problem was, he didn't wait for us to get out of the way on our two year olds. He nearly killed us instead. Maybe, that was his plan all along. The Italians I have worked with were precise in what they did. The Spanish not so, that's not to say that they aren't good at their jobs. The Brazilian's are grand, they are naturally good riders. The French are strange, but very good at the job. New Zealanders are like us Brits. The

Eastern Europeans are hard workers for the most part, and in many cases, hard drinkers. The Irish are special, they are a law unto themselves, the Welsh crack me up, I love their accent, and to my eternal shame, I can't understand anything the Scots say to me, it's not them, it's me. The one thing we all have in common is, we all share a love of horses and racing.

I shared a house with three Polish guys when I first moved to Lambourn. They taught me the meaning of hard drinkers. Strewth, they could put it away. Bottles of Polish vodka would slip down their throats, like a child eating jelly and ice cream. When they went on a bender, they got proper stuck in. I learnt to hide when the vodka came out, as I had to join in as well. They would practically force feed me their native food. With the best will in the world it wasn't that great. It just wasn't for me.

One of the Polish guys would go to bed when he had had enough, but the other would drink himself paralytic. He would be sat at the kitchen table, hanging on to the side, semi-conscious, till he passed out completely. More than once I had to get the guy in the house next door, to come and give me a hand to get the Pole out of the fireplace. He was a big man and I couldn't budge him. All our neighbour would to do when he walked in to the kitchen, was call out the Pole's name, softly I might add, and like magic, he would sit up straight for two seconds, then collapse again. How he didn't set himself on fire I will never know.

He had quite a sad story. He used to be a special policeman in Poland, he was highly trained. When it came to his retirement, his pension was practically nothing, certainly not enough to keep himself and his family. For whatever reason he couldn't get a job. So he packed up his car, his daughter decided to go with him. He left his wife behind, drove across Europe till he got to England, and ended up in Lambourn as a yard man. There you have it, a highly trained man, who shovels shit in a foreign country in order to survive. Never judge a book by it's cover, every one has their own story.

21

- 7 AND DROPPING

Lambourn in the snow is very pretty, unless you are working in it, or trying to get out of the Lambourn Valley of the Racehorse. It never seems to thaw once the white stuff has fallen. It probably doesn't help, that we start work so early whilst the temperature is still dropping. A balmy day was -7. The Jockey Club Estate guys work tirelessly from 4am, and sometimes earlier to keep the all weather gallops from freezing and therefore usable. Vaseline is often added to the all weather when it is laid, it helps to stop it hardening in very cold weather. Maddle Road, which has all the access points to the gallops, is salted continuously, to stop it from icing up, so the horses and riders have a reasonably safe surface to travel on. Yards with their own indoor rides can more or less carry on as usual. The only thing they can't do is do a piece of work.

At my yard, the worse bit, was walking the horses from the top yard, on the tarmac to the ride. The Polish yard men kept sweeping up the salt, saying it wasn't cold enough! Ice, says it's cold enough! We had to trudge, knee deep in snow across the field, with all our tack to get to the horses in the barn, as it was barely drivable. The horses in the bottom yard didn't get a look in as we couldn't get them out of the yard.

My boss had a plan, he contacted the trainer in the yard next door to our bottom yard, he was also an ex National Hunt jockey. Between them they took down the fence and cut a hole through the hedge, so that we could get the horses out for exercise in next doors all weather ride. Admittedly it was under rather a lot of snow, it wouldn't stop snowing!

On our first jaunt to use next doors ride, our horses waded elbow deep in snow, but they didn't care, they were glad to get out of their stables. Once in the ride we were able to walk, trot and canter, as the snow wasn't as deep, as it was in the field that we had travelled across. The horses worked hard. For once they didn't muck about, if one of the riders had fallen off, it would have been a soft landing, might have had to get a St Bernard dog to locate him, but that would have been part of the fun. Eventually, the snow did stop, and after a couple of weeks the temperature started heading towards 0. Happy days. Summer was a coming!

22

HEAD MAN

Reg our head lad was a wily old sort. Word had it that he was an ex jockey. He didn't miss a thing. He didn't ride out, he drove the yards Volvo up and down the gallops escorting the riders on their horses. He provided transport to the riders, by ferrying them and their tack in between the yards. There were quite a few staff with no transport, and their walking from yard to yard held us all up, not everyone who had a car wanted to give lifts to their fellow riders. We had a lot of horses to get through every morning. Most of us had between four to six lots to ride.

Reg started at silly o'clock. He had all the horses, in all six yards fed by 5.00am. We were to be sat on our first horse by 5.45am. When he had finished feeding, he would make his way back to main yard, park up and amble over to the houses where some of the staff lived. Then he would start calling out 'lovely day'. It could be pouring with rain, blowing a gale, a blizzard, but to him it was always 'lovely day'. If there was no response by 5.30am, he would go round knocking on the windows, calling out the names of those he knew couldn't get out of bed. If there was still no response he would go in the house and get them out. As I had been up since 4.20am to do my own horses, I used to meet him coming away from the houses grumbling under his breath about the lazy b******s.

He disliked a few people and didn't bother to hide it. Martin, one of the Polish guys who lived in my house, he was on Reg's hit list, he wouldn't come out of the house when Reg called him. Martin came out when, Martin was good and ready. He infuriated Reg no end.

Then there was the Indian Prince, or so he called himself. This lad could ride anything, and he reminded Reg of this fact at every available opportunity. He was always last in the ride first lot and last one back from breakfast. The rows they had, which would deteriorate rapidly with Reg threatening to sack him and cut his money as he was late, yet again. Everything Reg said, Mo returned, but with more eloquence which irritated Reg all the more. Brilliant to watch and listen to.

The two part time riders that Reg didn't like would egg Mo on, as it took Reg's attention away from them. Dean was another one who couldn't get of bed, but as he didn't live on site, Reg couldn't get at him. Rumour had it, that Dean had no less than five alarm clocks littered throughout his Flat to get him up on time and still he was late. He forgot everything, once he even forgot his hat. Reg was all for sending him home, the boss said 'no, we need him' and made Dean wear his daughters riding hat complete with pink hat silk. The other part timer just p****d Reg off the minute he set eyes on him in the morning. In fact, the boss and Reg would change the work board, that had the order of the horses to be ridden by this rider, the minute he had left the main yard with his tack. It got to the point, that whoever was riding out from the main yard, would check the board for changes, before we moved on to another yard, so we could tell him and anyone else, who's horse had been changed. So everyone was where they were supposed to be, they were sat on the right horse and ,if they had been playing musical horses, where the horse had been moved to.

I liked Reg, he was Welsh and made me laugh. He used to stand there in that tack room bouncing from foot to foot, smiling as the riders pulled faces over what they were going to ride. He would say 'Billie can ride anything'.

I would turn round and say 'but I don't want to ride just anything'. He had me married to one of the Christmas fillies that was an absolute tramp, even the jockeys on work days didn't want to sit on her. Thanks for that!

23

TWO YEAR OLDS

I liked the two year olds, although Monday mornings were a 'neck straps all the way chaps' scenario. I had my favourites they were mostly fillies. There was a dark bay filly with no white markings at all, she was called 'She Wants It'. She was the dead spit of my own mare. She was kind and was like shit off a shovel, my boss didn't pay her too much attention, so I had her all to myself. Another one I liked was a chestnut filly called Five Gold Rings, a friend of mine bought her a few years later to breed from her, she's thrown some nice foals by all accounts. She did like to fly leap at the bottom of the gallop, she was like a kangaroo. Super Academy was another chestnut, who was supposed to go to America but the deal fell through, I got on well with her. I found out that if you rode her like a National Hunt horse she was an easy ride.

I liked Christmas Came Twice, she was a tiny bay filly, I couldn't hold one side of her, so they put one of the lads on her one day. As we set off cantering, I was half expecting him to come sailing past me. When I turned round at the end of the gallop, he had only just managed to stay behind me. He was purple in the face from the effort of holding her. That made me feel a bit better, every time I rode this filly, I did a fly past most of the riders. Ladies Dancing was a nice bay colt with a perfect heart in the middle of his forehead, he had two speeds, but it depended on what leg he was on. On one leg his canter felt a bit laboured, then he would change to the other and he was suddenly turbo-charged.

I broke Pipers Piping, he was a bay colt. I didn't mean to, I had him tacked up and on his chain waiting to pull out, he had recently moved from the two year olds barn, to the big boys yard in the main yard. There was a tremendous crashing, followed by the sounds of thrashing around. The first crash was him wrapping his chain around his lower jaw. He then did a backward flip. He had broken his jaw. I got sent in disgrace to the vets, to have his jaw fixed. Turns out that he used to flip over when he was stabled in the barn, but nobody thought to say anything. Typical.

A filly I didn't like was by Monsieur Bond, she was a big bay filly, I tended to get her first thing in the morning whilst it was dark. She would leap and bronk most of the way whilst we were cantering on the gallop, my knuckles would be white from hanging on to the neck strap. More than once as we pulled up, the lad who was upsides me would comment, that they wouldn't want to be riding that in the dark. No shit! Neither did I. I got my own back on her one day, I was riding her in daylight for a change. As we went in to the indoor ride, she buggered about that much, she tripped and staggered a couple of strides. I took full opportunity of this and steered her in to one of the metal girders holding the roof up. I know that's not very nice of me, she was an absolute delight to ride that day. Clearly being concussed agreed with her.

And then there was that utter disease I was married to, courtesy of Reg. She was one of the Christmas fillies that I helped to pick up from the stud in my first week at this job. She was the one that wouldn't load. I had a feeling she was coming my way. She could whip round faster than the speed of light, her favourite place was at the entrance to the ride, but she could do it anywhere, any place, any speed. she should have been called Martini after the advert for the drink. I got rid of her on work days for while.

On Monday mornings, there would be the dreaded name Geese a Laying, next to my name. She would be awful, I spent quite a bit of time hanging round her neck. There was no point hitting her, it made her worse. One of the lads rode her one morning, she dumped him out the back door, off over her tail whilst going in the ride. He refused to ride her again. Wetty! Another lad rode her, and she dumped him so hard in the doorway to the ride, that he left a hole in the surface! When Christmas came, we had three days off. The lad Geese a Laying deposited outside the ride was acting head lad, this worked in my favour, as he put her on the walker, and left her there for the duration of morning and evening stables. His reasoning was, he was giving me a chance to stay on her when we returned to work. I was grateful to him. I never came off her, she wore me as a necklace a lot of the time, but I always managed to stay on board.

Lords a Leaping lived up to his name, he leapt every where. He was a handsome bay colt. He had this strange, straight legged gait when he went in to the ride. He only did it when he walked, being a colt, he was at the front of the string with the other colts, there was no need for the horny walk. As he got fitter, he became a bit of an arsehole, one of the part time riders put him firmly in his place with a couple of well aimed whacks, after he had reared so high, he was perilously close to going over backwards. Lords didn't do that again in a hurry, although he was still an arsehole to handle.

Sometimes, the two year olds could be a little tricky to get on, so having the right person to leg you up was important. Most of the yard staff were good at holding on to you, and the horse, if things started to unravel, and it looked like you were heading for an unplanned dismount. But Reg was ideal, he was always calm when things went tits up.

24

GOOD FRIDAY

Good Friday in Lambourn, is THE day for the race yards. The yards start at silly o'clock so that they have all their horses ridden, and the yard tidy, ready for visitors. This is the only day that the general public can go round the race yards that are open, meet the horses, and talk to the staff and trainers. Not all the yards open to the general public. There are displays of horses on the treadmills and swimming in the equine pools. The public aren't encouraged to see horses on the gallops as too many things can go wrong. Horses can spook easily and dump their riders, then you have a loose horse, and someone can get mowed down. Not ideal. The yards are only open in the morning.

In the afternoon, everyone moves to the Cricket Field, where there is various entertainment lined up for families, and other people. Racing staff don't have to be back at work till about 4pm, so they can enjoy the fun as well. Across the road, in between the Equine Valley Vets and the fibre sand gallop, there is a ring fenced off and a showjumping course put up. There is camel racing with the champion jockeys doing their best to pilot the camels. They also try their hand at jumping children's ponies, with mixed results and there is loads of good natured mickey taking. Nicky Henderson usually boxes a couple of his horses over from his yard at Seven Barrows, so that people can see horses close up, going over hurdles. Well known jockeys or ex jockeys are chosen to ride in this display. The beer tent is very well attended. In fact the pubs do a roaring trade on Good Friday, they put up marques, so that they can have bands and discos in them.

The first year I was in Lambourn, my boss decided he was going to open up one of our yards. The bottom yard would stay closed, so would the barn, but the main yard would be open. Then he changed his mind, put a chain on the gate to the main yard and locked it up. He allowed access to the square yard which housed a selection of yearlings, two year olds and 3 year olds. Reg was walking around shaking his head, muttering under his breath. I had come to understand, that was not a good omen. Then, we found out why. The boss sent the part time work riders home and told the rest of us that we would be doing a riding display on our gallop.

We were the only yard to be doing this. As my boss was a famous ex National Hunt jockey the place was packed out. We each had two lots to ride out in front of the public, thankfully I didn't have Geese a Laying, she would have done some damage to someone. I had my lovely She Wants It for the first run. We made our way to the open ring by the gallop, there were people everywhere and I mean everywhere. We circled, while our boss gave a small talk on each horse, then he sent me and Tim off first to do our canter. We started off okay, but as we came round the bend, WTF, our horses nearly came to a grinding halt. I have never seen so many people, they were all hanging over the white plastic rails, trying to see what was going on. The gap in the middle between the white rails had closed considerably. I gave my filly a hefty boot in the sides and urged her on, bless her heart, she carried on gamely, with Tim following close behind. We survived! On the way back down the track, we watched our fellow riders go through the same scenario. We had another lot to get out.

My next horse, Super Academy was up in the barn, so she was closer to the open ring. We all pulled out together, as we had decided that there was safety in numbers. Reg had gone home in disgust. This time, as we rode round the slaughter pit, the boss was charging people to sit in the back of his Discovery and travel upsides us, as we cantered. Talk about being the entrepreneur. Tim and I were first again, I was praying that Super wouldn't go in to a spin at the bottom of the gallop, as she could be prone to do, but she was a good girl, no spins that day. As Tim and I came round the bend we knew what to expect this time, so we had plenty of leg on, our horses had a look, put behaved like brave little soldiers.

Half way back down the track, we saw the second lot were coming up. The horse in front slammed on the brakes when he came round the bend. His rider urged him on, but as he drew level with the white railings, the horse ducked out to the side, how he didn't hit anybody was pure luck. The lad came off, right in front of the car. The horse buggered off, the boss slammed the brakes on to avoid running his rider over. All Tim and I could see, were the legs and feet of the people he had charged to sit in his car and watch the horses upsides, going up in the air, in the open boot, the tail gate was wide open and full of people. So much for health and safety. Then our boss took off after the horse, people fell out of the car boot, along with all the empty booze bottles and beer cans. It was complete carnage. Fortunately the lad was alright. A bit bruised and battered but in one piece. He was lucky. I wonder if the boss gave the money back to the people who were flung out of the back of the car. I bet he didn't, he had the gift of the gab. It wouldn't surprise me if he told them it was all planned and part of the act.

25

THE SOCIAL SCENE

It was a Good Craic in Lambourn. It had three main pubs, one was the Malt Shovel which has since been sold, that is situated between Lambourn and Upper Lambourn. The people who owned the Malt, sold up and moved to the George, which is slap bang in the middle of Lambourn. That was a god send, as then there were no more late night jaunts up the road in the pitch black, avoiding traffic and there were less drunk drivers on the road. Round the corner from the George, was a pub called The Wheelwright Arms. This was owned by an ex jockey. But I really liked the incredibly seedy Wine Bar, which was up the main street in Lambourn. It had the best, and I mean the best juke box ever! There was all sorts of music on it. You name it, it was on there. Loved it.

The Good Friday celebrations was a time for extreme excess for the stable lads and lasses. There were plenty of sore heads the following day, but everyone, well mostly everyone turned up for work in the morning. Those who didn't, got some serious bollockings and /or p*** taking. When the George was taken over, the new owners went to town making the festivities special, they did the same at Christmas and New Year. There are an awful lot of young people who have just come in to racing, they are away from their families, and they were having to fend for themselves. It can be a lonely time for them, but they usually make friends pretty quickly and racing becomes their new family. Everybody knows one another, this can be a good thing or a bad thing. Best to keep your nose clean and behave, word always got back to your boss if someone was a dick on a night out.

The people who had owned the Malt, put on different types of entertainment, once they hired a drag act. My daughter and myself went, mainly to see how this would go down. He/she went down a treat. He/she took the mickey out of the jockeys and the stable staff, he /she absolutely slaughtered us. His observations were spot on and we loved it. Let's be honest, most stable staff are relentless in making fun of each other and themselves, it's part of the job. The banter keeps us going, when you feel down, the weather is crap or when you are hanging off your horse throwing up last nights curry. At the end of the night, the drag queen who stood about 6'5" in his high heels, he towered over all of us. He spent much of his act stooped over, trying not to take his wig off in the beams above his head, announced, that he felt like he was in Lilliput. Brilliant!

New Years Eve is a busy night in Lambourn. The George sells tickets, so the only way to get in is to buy one. They have good entertainment, that's what you are paying for. One year I went to the Wheel as it was down the road from the house I rented. I went with a girl who lived with me. She was Scottish, I couldn't tell what she said and she could drink like a drain.

I left early for whatever reason, can't remember now. I was

in bed asleep, when I was woken with someone knocking on my front door. I staggered downstairs and opened the door to find myself looking at my lodger. One of the farriers had found her wandering round Lambourn, muttering to herself and had brought her home. Yes, she was so drunk she had no idea where she lived. She stood there on the doorstep, drooling, you read that right, she was actually drooling. How she had managed to stay upright, I will never know.

I somehow got her up the stairs and into her bed. She remained fully clothed. I was not going there, I got her a bucket and a glass of water and left her to it. By the time I had left her room she was unconscious. In the morning I got up as usual to do my horses before going to work, there was this burning smell that I could not track down. Eventually, I thought of my lodger. It went through my mind whether she was still alive, then I thought that maybe, the smell was coming from her room. YES to both. After knocking on her bedroom door for an age, I opened the door to a vision of her laid out like a corpse, snoring, under her duvet which was about to go up in flames. She had switched her hairdryer on, laid it on her bed whilst it was still going, because she was cold and then passed out again. I had gas central heating and it was turned on! I really wanted to kill her, but as she was already half dead, it would have been a bit of overkill.

26

LAMBOURN AND HELEN

There were a few good times my daughter and myself fell out of the Malt. I lived a mile in one direction and she lived a mile in the opposite direction. As we shared my car, after a night out it was pot luck who drove who home, kept the car and did the horses in the morning. This time we had both drunk too much, we argued about who was driving, standard for us. We staggered across the road to the car park, she announced that she was driving, I unlocked the car, and she got in the passenger seat, the side with no steering wheel. While she was wondering where the steering wheel was, I got in the other side feeling rather smug. We set off towards the village and Helen's home. Besides her house there was a car park which was for the Catholic church. I drove in alright, but we couldn't find the gate that took her to her house, we drove round and round that car park, laughing like a pair of hyenas. Eventually she got out, I returned home, cautiously, I might add. I was up at my usual time, our own horses were done and I was sat on my first horse by 5.45am. I have always had a knack for sobering up in two minutes Flat, I have been very glad of that at times.

When I finally managed to rent a house in Lambourn, they are like rocking horse shit to find. I enlisted Helen's help with retrieving my furniture from Sparkford in Somerset. I had put my belongings into storage when I left there nearly a year previously...

I hired a van, and we set off singing very badly to the songs on the radio. Sparkford is along the A303, I hate driving along that road. Why does all the traffic slow down at Stonehenge? The stones don't move around, they don't change colour. I don't get it, and especially on a cold November afternoon. By the time we arrived at Sparkford roundabout it was dark, we were about to pull off at the first exit, when lo and behold, Queen's Bohemian Rhapsody came on the radio. Well, there was no way we were going to pass up on murdering that song, we drove round that roundabout doing all the head movements until the song finished, then, we pulled in to Sparkford storage, loaded up, and travelled back to Lambourn. Traffic was still slow by the dreaded Stonehenge. We dumped everything in my house, I took the van back to the rental place in Newbury to pick up my car. Another, extremely long day completed.

Not long after that I went 'airmail' on the gallop, I broke my leg and ankle again. I spent the rest of that winter, riding and leading our two mares all over the Downs, with my leg in plaster and a plastic carrier bag tied to my foot to keep it dry. Helen did the mucking out and I did riding, until the weather got warmer, then the mares were turned out. That was another very cold, snow laden winter. My little terrier used to come with me when I rode, until I spotted a couple of Buzzards circling overhead eyeing him up for dinner, then he couldn't come any more.

Both my daughter and myself drove my car, our horses had

been moved to a farm up Maddle Road, thankfully before the snow and ice arrived. We needed to go to Wantage one day after morning stables, the main road was closed, due to snow drifts and ice. So we decided to go cross country. The farmers around Lambourn do their best to keep the roads open. It really hit home, just how much it had snowed, when we turned down a lane, a tractor had made it's way down this lane, pushing the snow out of the way. It was a single track, with a solid wall of snow and ice towering either side of us. If the car had broken down, we would have been unable to get out to find help. If the snow had come tumbling down we would have been buried until it thawed. We made it to Wantage and back again, good old Peugeot.

Another time going to Wantage we ran out of diesel. There was that horrible chugging, spluttering noise going on, so we did what any sane people would do. We started doing the rocking movements to get us a little further to our destination, we got about ten feet. There are no petrol stations in Lambourn, the nearest place is Membury services who charge extortionate prices for everything. We thought we would make it to Wantage, we got that well and truly wrong. Thankfully we had our phones on us, and reception, another plus, Helen put a status on Facebook, asking if anyone was near us and if so could they pick us up some diesel.

Thankfully Facebook didn't let us down, and a friend of ours turned up to take us to a petrol station. And yes, the car started first time when it had juice in it. Result!!

A few years later, we went to pick up a cooker we had bought, we were about to move in to a house at Woodside. We were waiting for the woman to come home, so we could pay for and load the cooker in to the car. She walked up the road to see us two singing very badly, to a Marilyn Manson CD. God only knows what she must have thought of us!

27

FFOS LAS

Ffos Las is quite a new racecourse. It was built at site of a coal mine after mining had finished there. The racecourse opened on 18th June 2009. My boss at the time, was determined to have a runner on the first day. The only problem was, we were mainly a Flat yard with no jumpers in residence. This did not deter my determined boss. He scoured the four year olds until he found a suitable candidate. Ta Da!!! He found his prospective hurdler in the shape of a nearly black horse called Ted's Fantasy.

Ted wasn't that fantastic on the Flat, but his hurdling training began forthwith. A jockey was located to ride the horse and help get him jumping. I was a little disappointed with the choice of jockey, but it wasn't my decision. The boss was a very good rider, riding was effortless. On the first day of training, I was roped in to go and get another trainers hack, to lead the way for Ted. This horse was for the boss to ride over the hurdles. Well in my book, my boss showed the other jockey up, he was stylish and met every hurdle correctly. The jockey, bearing in mind that the horse he was sat on was a novice, looked like a monkey shagging a log. Ted took to jumping quickly and easily. After a couple of sessions, he was declared fit to run on the first day at Ffos Las.

On the day in question Ted was loaded up in the box, one of the secretaries who rode out took him. My boss finally had a runner over the jumps, fitting, as he had been a very successful National Hunt jockey. The horse didn't win but it was the taking part that counted.

Not long after, Ted was sold to another National Hunt trainer up the road from us. This horse was a bit of a rebellious sort. The new trainer had him gelded and rode him himself. Within a couple of weeks the horse was unrecognisable, he was a completely different horse. He was calm and responsive to his rider, never saw that before. But when you watched how he was being ridden, he was ridden to suit the horse. The new trainer had clearly taken the time to work out how to ride Ted, instead of just getting on him and p*****g the horse off. Every horse has a key, and it's worthwhile taking the time to find out how each one ticks. Saying you don't have the time, there are too many horses to ride, is no excuse. You want that horse to work to the best of his of her ability. You, as the rider are sat on these horses everyday for up to an hour, surely you can take the time to work out how to ride them successfully. Granted there are those horses that no matter how hard you try, you just don't get on with them and the dislike is mutual.

28

A DIFFERENT YARD

I changed yards. I was plain knackered from getting up at 4.20 every morning. I went back to a National Hunt yard, they start later in the morning. The yard itself was easier, all the barns were in the same place. I had forgotten how much bigger National Hunt horses were. As I was the smallest and lightest rider, I got to ride the horses with the bad backs. Lucky me. This generally entailed them being ridden in GP saddles rather than race saddles. I found out that I couldn't actually ride as short as I needed to, on the gallop in a GP saddle. The knee rolls got in the way.

I didn't like it there, but if you don't try it, you don't know. It finished me off when I was expected to ride a young horse who was tightly strapped down with an elastic bungee. The poor thing was very sore in his neck and mouth, another bad back in the making. I got off him half way round his walking exercise and took the bungee off. I got some telling off for that, I found another job pronto.

Over a year later, whilst I was working part time for various people, I returned to this yard. I was working for a showjumper, one of the barns had been let out to her. She had less 'gadgets' than this racehorse trainer, made me laugh, that did.

I did some office work there, after I had completed the British Racing School Racing Secretary course. Then I realised that there are very few secretary jobs going, so that was a waste of time. Ah well!!

29

COMPTON

After leaving the National Hunt yard in Upper Lambourn, I started a job as a stable lass, about two miles from Lambourn in a pretty chocolate box village called Compton. It was a mixed yard.

Most of the trainers in Lambourn, and the surrounding villages have what is known as a combined licence, it means that they can train horses for both the Flat and National Hunt races. There is a difference in training these horses. Although a fit horse, is a fit horse. A lot depends on the distance. Slow horses are aimed at longer distance races, in the hope that stamina will play a part and they get placed. Hopefully they are not still running two days later (in the same race, but are really truly slow). The speed merchants (sprinters) are aimed for the shorter races. A good trainer will find a race for a horse to run well in. Some horses like certain racecourses, The ground that they run on plays a very big part in how a horse will perform on the day. Some like heavy going, some prefer hard ground, some like dirt tracks, some like all weather surfaces. The trainer has to know what every horse he has in his yard, prefers to run on. Everyone would love their horse to be able to run on good ground, something with a bit of cut in it, so the horse can get a grip with each stride.

My time working in Compton was interesting to say the least. My new boss and his wife were genuinely nice people. The stable yard itself was very old. Proper red brick buildings with floors that were permanently wet when it rained, the other half of the yard were wooden built stables and dry! There were ten of each.

My boss Alan, used to rave about his lovely legs, why I don't know, but racing is full of eccentric people. After every lot, either he would make a brew or get one of us to make it, and it was served on the patio table outside his house. When it was cold, the mugs would freeze to the metal table, then the race was on, to get your tea down your neck before it got cold.

There were times that I was in abject misery with the wet and the cold, I began to wonder if racing was still what I wanted to do. We mucked our stables out, in to large plastic bins. Then we had to carry the heavy plastic muck bins around to the muck trailer. As the yard was small and quaint, there wasn't enough room for a ramp to wheel a wheelbarrow on to the trailer. It wasn't too bad when it was dry, but when it was wet, the bedding and shit stuck to you, all you could smell was horse pee. As winter wore on, Tesco was starting to look very enticing. Then something would happen that I found very funny and all was well again.

There were only Jan, the head girl, Alan, the boss, a yardy, who's name I have forgotten, one other girl and myself. Four of us to ride out. Often a couple of jockeys from Lambourn would come to ride out if they were a bit short on money, or when we had a horse going racing. This would leave us short staffed on the yard. We only had twenty horses in training, but take Alan, someone to drive the lorry, usually Jan, and the person who would lead the horse up at the racecourse, it left us a bit thin on the ground especially for evening stables.

Our nearest gallop was Long Hedge, the Jockey Club looked after it, even though it was a couple of miles away from the Mandown Gallops. We had approximately a mile of riding along the main road, to get from our yard to Long Hedge. Most of the time it passed without incident, but a lot of people drive too fast, and were shocked to see a small string of racehorses on the road. It was especially bad when the sun was low, and the roads were wet, we could see on our horses, but the drivers were often blinded by the sun, and the glare from the wet tarmac. I lost count of the amount of times our horses nearly went through the barb wire fence on our left, to try to get out of the way of speeding vehicles.

The surface at Long Hedge was woodchip, when it was dry, it was dusty, when it was wet, it was soggy and dead. There was no bounce to help the horse along. You feel every step the horse makes, it vibrates up through the shoulders. One of my horses was a little colt, he suffered from sore shins. He wouldn't have been the fastest of horses with good shins, but I do think that his sore shins could have been avoided by taking him to Mandown, to make use of the various surfaces available.

30

OWNERS DAY

What I liked about Alan was that he cared about his horses, they weren't just seen as a meal ticket, and he cared about his owners. He was very aware that without the owners, there would be no horses. So every Saturday, he had his owners in to watch their horses on the gallop, and to talk in person, to say how they were getting on with their training and when they were likely to run.

What I wasn't so keen on was the red polo shirt with my bosses name on it. They only came in one size. HUGE. When I stood up, the hem fell to my knees, the shoulders were at my elbows. I would try to take as much material up inside my body protector, hoping it would stay there and not escape! Then, there was the jacket. The jacket wore me, it filled up with air when we hit the gallop. I was the only cantering bright red tomato. I truly was a sight to behold!

We, the riders, would ride round the yard, whilst Alan gave his short talk on each horse and rider. Thankfully it didn't last long, small yard etc... The entertaining bit was waiting for him to get to Claire, he always faltered, glared at her, assessing how drunk she was and then carried on.

Claire had lost most of her nerve riding, she loved her job. Instead of saying, 'I'm nervous about riding,' she hit the bottle, to give her some courage. Alan would have gladly given her a job on the yard, but she thought that was beneath her. Unfortunately, a lot of riders think like this and hope that no one notices. We all lose our nerve at some time, most of us get it back, but some don't.

A couple of extra people would come in to ride out on Saturday mornings, which was nice and they enjoyed the attention of the owners. We always hoped with extra riders that we would finish a bit earlier. We were so wrong.

The owners would drive up to Long Hedge, quite few of them had their vehicles full of other horse owners, there was always a nice atmosphere. They would take photos of their horse on the gallop, and a big red tomato.

There was only one toilet on the yard, when the owners were there it could be a bit awkward. Often there was a queue, they let us riders push in front of them, there was no lock on the door. There was no point in singing, as no one would hear, you just hoped that some one was standing guard. I was in there one time and this bloke walked straight in. I don't know who was more surprised, him or me, as my voluminous red polo shirt hit my knees. I was quite pleased of it that day.

31

MANDOWN

On work days, which in most racehorse yards are Tuesdays and Fridays, we would box to Mandown, to mainly use the Short and the Long gallops. There are other gallops there with turf and most forms of artificial surfaces. There are different gradients and lengths, starting with flat and progressing to fairly steep hills to train on. There is the grass area known as the bowl, below the National Hunt and hurdle fences, as the name suggests, horses and their riders work round this for however many circuits. Fences are on both turf and artificial ground. There are training fences from train sleepers, to get young horses jumping, all the way up to Grand National fences. A trainer can find a surface to train practically any horse on. It is an ideal place to train horses, anyone can use these facilities so long as they pay a levy to the Jockey Club, although it would be best not to go there in the morning, if you are not training a racehorse. So Dora, The Explorer after paying your fee, don't be surprised when you are shouted at and overtaken at speed, because you are hogging the gallop at a trot, yes it does happen. You need to get out of the way pretty fast!

Our lorry was a converted bread van, it could transport three horses. But it still looked like a bread van, not a vehicle designed to carry lean, mean, racing machines. There was usually Alan, Jan and myself. Jan, drove the lorry most of the time, Alan supervised, much to her annoyance, he might as well have drove it himself. We were only three miles away from Mandown, but the mood by the time we got there could be thunderous.

Alan usually rode when we went to Mandown, Jan sometimes rode, but it depended on what we took. I was always saddled with a chestnut mare called Flying Free, she was a sly mare, always dropping her left shoulder, and then trying to whip round. I would follow Alan on to the Short, where we would do a steady canter till the end, then we would trot on the grass down to the three furlong marker on the Long. That bloody mare would play up stepping down on to the gallop, dropping her shoulder, and generally being an arse. It was made more difficult, because Alan didn't know his left from his right.

Our conversation on the way to the Long would be, 'I want you on my right' whilst pointing with his left hand.

I would say 'that's your left'.

He would then say, flapping left his arm about 'I know my left, from my right, I want you on this side, on my right'.

Then I would say, 'you mean your other right?'. By this time, I would be swearing over the mare as she side stepped all over the place, trying to keep the tramp straight, with my knees under my chin. Once she was on the gallop she was alright. Alan would still be going on about his right and lefts, I was to join him at the six furlong marker where our two horses would work together.

The journey home was a quiet affair, where we didn't speak, we thought about how our horses worked and whether it could have gone any differently.

32

JUMPING DAYS

We had a few jumpers, one of the stars of the yard, was a dappled grey mare called Kijvou, she was a good looking mare and quite good at her job. There was a nice old fashioned Thoroughbred mare, who didn't have the best conformation for racing. She had a long neck, a big head, with a high head carriage, and a long back, that was starting to dip in the middle. She was only about 16hh, but she had a heart of gold and tried her hardest to please. She rode big, you felt like you were sat on a 17hh horse. I only rode her once at Mandown, I disgraced myself totally on her.

On jump days, Alan would arrange to meet one of our usual jockeys at the lorry park, where the tractors, and the other equipment for looking after the gallops was stored. Visiting yards who had boxed over would park here. He would then jump in the jockeys car as he wasn't riding, drive up to the cross road on the gallop, where the Long passes by, the Short ends and Fishers Hill ends. There is another car park there for trainers and owners to watch their horses.

He would wait for the jockey and myself to canter along the

Short, get to the end, then go down to three furlong marker on the Long, and work through to the end of that gallop. We then headed to the schooling ground. He often drove the jockeys car right up to the schooling ground, much to their disgust. They wanted the rides on Alan's horses, so they said nothing about it, but did plenty of muttering under their breaths. Sometimes they took their car keys with them, jumped on their horse and made haste to the Short, leaving Alan no choice but to drive the bread van up to the crossroad. But he never drove his lorry along the path to the schooling ground. He would rather walk.

By the time we arrived at the schooling ground our horses were nicely warmed up. I had decided by this stage in my career, that my days of schooling over hurdles and fences, were well and truly over. The horse that the jockey was sat on would jump first, then we would swap horses and he would jump mine. The jockeys liked to ride the horses they were going to be riding in a race beforehand, it gave them an insight as to how the horse would perform on the day.

The first horse jumped well. I was on the old fashioned Thoroughbred mare, she decided that she didn't want to play ball. I had already struggled to see where I was going on the two gallops we had cantered on. I was too small to see between her ears, so I rode her to one side, looking over her shoulder. A periscope was what was needed.

Before we could swap horses, she went in to reverse. The schooling ground has a really tall, thick hedge to one side of it. I found out that it wasn't thick enough to stop a determined horse from going through it. One moment I was sat there, with my reins like washing lines, watching the other horse jump and the next, well, we were going backwards. As there weren't any other horses waiting to use the schooling ground, I wasn't really worried. My feeble attempts at trying to motivate the equine version of a passenger liner in to going forward didn't work. It wasn't until we had backed up to the hedge, that I started to think something might be amiss. At this point Alan noticed that I wasn't were I should be and started yelling at me.

'Where are you going?'

My answer of 'through the hedge….backwards' didn't go down well. I couldn't blame him, I would have yelled at me. I was about to be violated by a hedge and there was nothing I could do about it. Four wheel drive was engaged as she reversed in to the hedge. All my kicking was to no avail, she was in the middle of the foliage and quite content about it. Alan had to pull us out, whilst berating me (deservedly) on my lack of steering skills. All I could do was giggle.

I swapped horses with the jockey, and my mare ducked, and dived at all her fences. The jockey called her every name under the sun, whilst picking bits of hedge out of her mane and tack.

I think it fair to say, that I was not employee of the week. I laughed all the way back to the box and we drove home in silence, well he did, I was still laughing at myself. Yet another occasion, where my sense of humour has let me down!!

33

JAN

Every now and then, Jan would ride one of the horses that had been boxed to Mandown, she usually got jocked off, and a jockey would take her place. If this was going to happen, the jockey would be waiting at the crossroad. Alan would be there to leg the jockey up. Down in the lorry park we would have one of the muck bins to stand on, so that we could vault on our horse. Well I did, so did Alan, Jan needed legging up. A job for Alan that was.

Alan had cadged a lift with his jockey, who was short on time, he was riding in a race later on that day. Jan rode the horse along the Short, then, swapped with the jockey at the crossroad. Alan wasn't riding that day, so a huge sigh of relief, I wasn't going to have the right/left argument. We, the jockey and myself received our instructions and set off for the Long. As we cantered pass the crossroad on our horses, I looked across to see that Jan and Alan were having one of their arguments. They missed us riding past, waste of time being there. They might as well have been married, but Alan already had a wife.

We pulled off the gallop and made our way back to the crossroad. Alan had stomped off to sit in the lorry. He didn't even wait to hear how the horses had travelled, he must have been really angry. Jan was waiting for the horse. The crossroad is quite a busy place, there are horses and riders constantly passing either on the gallops, or on the walkways. The riders do not miss a trick. They had already clocked the argument between Alan and Jan, they had also clocked the jockeys car and that he would be leaving pronto. The antenna had gone up that something was about to happen….

The jockey dismounted, and prepared to leg Jan up. All movement around us stopped. Before I go any further, Jan was a larger lady, quite a few in National Hunt are a bit bigger than the average rider. But Jan has no, and I mean no, spring in her. If someone is legging you up, the least you can do is to meet them halfway by having some spring. You are going up quite a way, you can not expect anyone to lift nine or ten stone, or even more in some cases, from the ground to a destination that is six foot, or above in the air.

The first attempt to get Jan on board was half successful, if she had jumped when she was first hoisted in the air, she would have been there. Admittedly it was rather a tall horse she was getting on.

After the failed first attempt, there were calls of 'nearly there', and 'there you go', followed by 'oooh', and 'weh-hey' More efforts were made to get her on board, after each attempt, she slid back down the side of the horse, like jelly had been thrown at a wall. The poor woman didn't know where to put herself. The jockey was sweating, and blowing, and running out of energy. Jan decided in the end (thank god), to walk the horse back to the lorry. She had to endure the walk of shame along the walkways, with the other strings sniggering at her. It wasn't fair, admittedly it was very funny to watch, but she didn't deserve to be humiliated like that. The mood in the lorry was EPIC.

34

RAINING CATS AND DOGS

I wasn't the only one, who had displeased Alan, to the point of being him getting narky. Although, I did annoy him quite often, more so than the other staff. After my episode with the hedge, I mainly rode the Flat horses. My little colt was struggling with the surface at Long Hedge. He was always getting left behind, as he was sore, I would go easy on him, I got away with this when, it was just Claire and myself riding out together. The colt was along way off from running in a race. He was slow as a boat, and was never going to set the world of horse racing alight. He was not a racehorse, his thing was eating, that was all he cared about. I met his owner a few years later, he had had a couple of runs and finished at the back each time, so they took him home to eat.

Going back home one day after his exercise, Claire was in front of me. We were trotting on the main road, one of his front shoes flew off in front of her. We were both pretty impressed with this. We hadn't gone another ten yards, when the other one flew off across the road. Of course we found this very funny and chuckled all the way home. Alan lost his rag that night at evening stables, both Jan and himself checked all the horses legs and feet every single night, but I got the blame for not informing him that the colts shoes were loose. I gave up after that!

It was yet another cold, damp day, we were on route to Mandown. We had two horses on the lorry ready to go, but three were down on the board to go to Mandown. Enter Fergus, the jockey. He thought that we were going to meet him at the gallops, but no, he had obviously displeased the boss in some way. As Fergus had no rides in a race that day, Alan had made him drive to the yard. Jan and myself made room for him in the lorry. Again no, Fergus was going to be riding his horse to Mandown. The forecast was for torrential rain at some point in the morning. Alan didn't care, he told Fergus he had better get a move on, as we were supposed to be working together on the Long.

We passed him on the main road, Jan and I felt sorry for him, I offered to ride the horse there and Fergus get a lift in the lorry. Alan was driving and wouldn't stop. Obviously, we were way ahead of Fergus, so our horses had a pick of grass before we got on, whilst waiting. When he turned up, we made our way to the usual gallops, to do our usual thing. All those facilities and we only used the same gallops. Doh!! After our work was done, Fergus started to make his way home. We had just loaded up the horses, when the heavens opened, and I mean opened. The weather forecast was not lying, I shall never forget seeing Fergus walking on his horse along the road by Wicks, the saddlers. Talk about drowned rats. After we had arrived back at the yard, we unloaded the horses and tack. Jan and I were going to go back for him and the horse, but Alan said 'no'. We never found out what had gone on between them, but whatever it was, must have been pretty serious. It took Fergus about an hour to get back home, he refused to trot his tired horse.

35

GOING RACING

I went racing quite a bit at Alan's. I was lucky enough, that the horses I looked after, were ready to run. And although it was a much smaller yard, the racing tack room was much better organised.

The first time I went racing with this yard, I took a gelding who was quite highly thought of. We went to the dreaded Goodwood, although this time it was a lot easier for me as I wasn't travelling head lass. I spent the time leading up to the race, pulling my horses mane and generally making him a handsome boy, but not handsome enough. We didn't win best turned out.

We went to Lingfield quite a bit, the only remarkable thing to happen there, was on a windy day in the stables, the buckets were faster than the horses.

At Kempton we got excited as a top jockey had been booked to ride my horseVendetta. We weren't quite so thrilled when, it became obvious that he couldn't hold the horse and came back grinning, saying 'it had been some time since he was last run off with'. I think Alan wanted to kill him!

A visit to Bath racecourse was a little more exciting. The lad who had his horse stabled opposite me, lost his horse in the lake. It got away from him and went for a swim. It was his first time racing, I wonder if he went again?

When Vendetta ran at Doncaster, Jan and I thought that Alan would get a lift there with Ven's owner Paul. But no, he came in the lorry with us and for once we had a good time. The radio was playing full blast and all three of us were singing along to the songs. Then Snow Patrol came on, Jan and I found out that Alan had learnt to play the drums at school. Why was he training racehorses when he could be in a band? This turned out to be a memorable trip to Donny.

Paul, the horses owner, turned up as the race was about to begin. The horses were on their way down to the start, when it was announced that there was a hitch on the racecourse. All sorts or things were going through our minds, had someone come off? Had a horse pulled a shoe? Had a horse misbehaved in the stalls? We looked up at the big TV screen which was across the racecourse, opposite the parade ring. Sailing past, flat out, was a horse and jockey, thankfully not ours. The race commentator did what he was paid to do, he commented for the duration of the jockey being bolted with. The cameras did their best to keep up with the runaway, as they came flying past the parade ring a huge cry went up, like they had won The Gold Cup at Cheltenham. When they went past the finishing post, the jockey managed to pull up, jumped off the horse, threw the reins at the stable lass and stormed off to the weighing room. The race then started and normal service was resumed, our horse finished in the middle of the field.

The drive home was another memorable event. Alan decide to ride home with Paul. Most of the way home, he made Paul sit behind us, just so he could keep phoning Jan, to tell her how badly she was driving the lorry. Things like; you are wandering about, she wasn't. You have gone over the white line on the motorway, she was overtaking. You didn't indicate correctly. I ended up answering the phone as Jan was driving. Alan kept telling me to pass the phone over to Jan, so he could speak to her in person. Jan didn't want to speak to him in person, I had to relay his gripes.

When she pulled in to a services to get diesel, he pulled in behind her, and phoned from the car. He could just have easily have got out and told her face to face that, she hadn't indicated in plenty of time, to say that she was coming off the motorway, and she wasn't filling the diesel tank up correctly. When she ignored him, he finally got out of the car, strode up to her and started to tell her all over again. Big mistake, big, big mistake, how he didn't end up with the pump hose wrapped round his head I will never know. Everyone was looking at them, She was screaming at him to drive his own bloody lorry, and that she would go home with Paul in the car. I was very selfish, inwardly pleading that this wouldn't happen. Before she could make good her threat, Alan turned tail, got back in to the car and told Paul to drive on. As we pulled out of the services we half expected that Paul and Alan would be waiting in a lay by for us to pass. But no, there was no sign of them and we drove home in peace. When we arrived home, we thought that Alan would come out in to the yard to start again, but he was a no show. Thank god.

36

PAUL

Paul was what is known as a hands on owner. He kept in regular contact with the yard, he was very involved with his horses upkeep. He was an ex jockey, who also owned a couple of other horses with another trainer. He moved one of his horses, Fearless Kenny to our yard for training, he was a nice horse. Then, not long after, Vendetta turned up, then came Star. Star was his baby. Paul would come in, to ride out his own horses, as much as he could.

Despite being an ex jockey, his riding wasn't that stylish. There was one day, we were cantering up Long Hedge gallop, Paul was in front, he was squadron leader that day. It was quite foggy, we gradually lost sight of Paul and Star as they pulled away from us. We, the riders, kept at a steady pace, as we had been told. As we got near the top, we were expecting to see Paul and Star on their way back down the hill, but on the grass that ran alongside the gallop. There was no sign. We got to the end of the gallop, our horses spooked. There in the field, directly in front of us, was a large florescent blob coming out of the mud. That'll be Paul then. No sign of Star. He had buggered off with Paul, Star didn't stop at the end, but carried on, dumping Paul on the way. A neighbouring trainer found the horse wandering along a path, safe and sound. Paul went to pick him up later that day.

As Paul became more successful in his daytime job, he bought more horses. He put them all with Alan. I couldn't believe it when he bought Pipers Piping, he was the 3year old colt who's jaw was broken when I put him on his chain, in his stable at Upper Lambourn. He had been gelded in the mean time and could now, be safely tied up without him doing his backward flips. Winning!!

The only thing with having one major owner in a yard was, and probably still is, is that, if things go wrong, and they either can't or won't pay their training fees, the trainer is in deep trouble. There is no money coming in to pay the staff, farrier, vet and the other bills. Even more so, if the owner is Irish. They can go back home to Southern Ireland, where they are not obliged to pay the debts, that they have run up here in England.

In Paul's case, he started to run out of money, he had twenty horses in training. You have to be a multi millionaire, to be able to afford twenty horses in training. He found a yard of his own, moved his horses there, so that he could train them himself. Which worked for a while. He had a genuine love for his horses.

I had started my Equine Massage training by then, he very kindly allowed me to use his horses, any of his horses, for the practical assessments that I had to submit to gain my qualification. In return, when he was racing or working, I would do his evening stables. I was recovering from a broken leg, so this arrangement worked out well for us. I skipped out, hayed, watered and fed the horses that hadn't gone racing. Paul was decent with me and I respected him for that. He did the majority of the yard work. He employed an apprentice jockey, who a lot of people slagged off, but from what I saw, she worked bloody hard. She would muck out eighteen horses on her own, first thing in the morning and never complained about it.

A few years later, I heard that he had lost his yard, and had sold most of his horses, he still had Star, and a couple of others, that he had managed to hang on to. Unfortunately, he had run up huge debts, and had to leave the village. He was a betting man, as so many are in racing. He was addicted to horse racing, it was his life. Then his life took a sinister turn when he started to defraud people. He got caught out, and is serving a prison sentence. Bloody idiot.

37

BREAKING MY LEG AGAIN

Claire and myself shared the big chestnut mare called Flying Free, that name turned out to be rather apt in my case, when I went airmail on the gallop at Long Hedge. I got to ride this mare every work day. Joy! The days in between, Claire rode her. Why Claire couldn't ride her on work days was beyond me. She loved the mare and I disliked this horse a lot. As I mentioned before, the horse was a brat, if she couldn't have her own way, she would have a tantrum.

Things came to a head one day as we came back from the gallop, we used to cut through a little road, which ran adjacent to the main road. It meant that we didn't spend as much time on the main road dodging traffic, and it was a little bit quicker. On this road, there were a few houses, one of which kept a standard poodle as a pet. It hated the horses going past his house, his owners mostly kept the dog in the house, until we had finished morning stables. On this day, the dog was loose in the garden when we came back from exercise. As soon as it clocked us, he came running up to the fence, barking and flinging himself against the gate. As usual, Free took matters in to her own hands, she started to kick out at the gate, getting closer and closer. Claire did nothing but sit there. Alan lost his rag, got off his own horse, and dragged Free away from the gate, before she kicked it to pieces and serious trouble set in for all of us. Thankfully the dog didn't escape. Alan vowed that Claire would not be riding the mare again.

Next day comes along, guess what? I've got that damn horse. But, I wasn't down to ride her with the string, I was going out on her with one of the jockeys who had come in to ride out. As we left the yard, heading in the direction of Long Hedge, Alan followed us out in to the road, he said to 'do what I had to', if she played up. He hated his horses being hit, he was really ticked off with the whole situation. As soon as Alan went back in the yard, the mare started to play up, dropping her left shoulder, trying to spin round, then she attempted to put herself on the floor. She received two of the biggest whacks across her shoulder, the offending side. The jockey offered to swap horses, I refused, I was determined to make that damn mare behave herself. Fair play to her, all it took was the two well aimed whacks and she did behave herself. In fact she led all the way along the road to Long Hedge, and, she continued to lead on the gallop. She was foot perfect. Dare I say, I enjoyed riding her. Never thought I would say about Free, but there you go. This was a horse that wouldn't lead on the road, traffic was used by her, as target practice. She would look for something to kick, she didn't care if it was a car, cyclist or lorry. In her mind they were all fair game. She certainly did not lead on the gallop, she would rather drop you. Anywhere and didn't care.

When we got back and reported how she had behaved, Alan was really pleased. I got her again the next day, Claire complained about it. I went to Alan, and said 'if I'm sorting this mare out, I'm keeping her, until Claire can ride the horse properly'. I was absolutely sick of being given horses who could be difficult to handle and ride. They are made like that in most cases; because the trainers, the assistants and head lads don't want to offend the riders, who are making a pigs ear out of riding certain horses. Offend away I say, if I can't ride something I say so, find another rider who can do a better job. What is sickening is, when you have worked hard on a horse regaining his trust. You get him going right, only for the horse to be given back to the rider, who had caused the problem in the first place. Then you watch, as all your hard work goes down the drain, and the horse comes back to you worse than ever. This is how some horses get a bad name.

A day or so later, I was down to ride Free in the string up to the gallop at Long Hedge. I had Claire in front of me on a little horse, moaning away, about her not riding Free. She had clearly forgotten that, the only horse on the yard that, she could actually ride, at the time, was the one she was sat on. Jan was behind me, I would have preferred to be in front, the constant whinging was doing my head in. Maybe being squadron leader would shut her up. I stayed in the middle.

We set off very slowly on the gallop, to the point that Free was still trotting when we went past the two marker, both myself and Jan shouted for her to go on a stride, eventually she did and we hit canter. No sooner had we started cantering, than Free started to fly buck and twist in the air. Again, I shouted to Claire to go on a stride, but it was like talking to a brick wall. She was determined to be as difficult as possible. We hit the three furlong marker, I was launched in the air. I had asked AGAIN, for Claire to go on a stride. I was on the right hand side about to over take her, when I parted company with Free, cleared Claire and horse she was sat on, and landed on my feet, on the grass at the side of the gallop. The ground was frozen, I had deja vu from a few years previously, as I keeled over and sat on my ass. Great.

Then, even better!! A pair of red bandages appeared in front of me, attached to pair of chestnut legs. As Free stood over me, she looked down, I was convinced that she was going to trample me, all I could think of was that, this is really going to hurt. But I swear Free laughed, as she turned and ran after her mates on the gallop, who were in the process of being wrestled back under control. It had all gone tits up for Jan, as her horse almost planted her as well. She managed to pull up and to be honest, I wasn't that interested in where Claire ended up. Harsh I know.

38

THE TRIP

Jan always had a phone on her in case of emergencies, I suppose this was one of those times. I didn't see me getting back on a horse any time soon. Alan arrived quite quickly, with one of the jockeys who had come in to ride out. The jockey was put on Free to take her home.

It was yet another foggy day and despite having Hi Vis on, Alan still managed to nearly drive over the top of me. FML could this day get any worse? Yes, is the answer to that. Alan picked me up to put me in the front of the Discovery, he tripped, luckily I still had my hat on, or else I would have headbutted the door with my head instead of my hat. Then I would have been admitted to hospital with a concussion, as well as everything else. Once placed in the car, he decided that I needed something to rest my leg on. He rummaged around in the back of the car for a while and came back with a toolbox. Yes, you read that right, my leg that was broken in three places was balanced on a toolbox, all the way to Swindon hospital.

Bless him, his heart was in the right place. We had a discussion about which way to go, would it be best to go to the Royal

Berkshire, John Radcliffe or Swindon. Neither of us knew which one would be best, so I said the nearest.

I think he hit every pothole in the road and then some, on way to Swindon. By the time we got there I couldn't speak. People who know me, would say this a rarity. He abandoned the Discovery in the car park of A&E, to go in search of a wheelchair. I was surprised to see him returning with one, it had gone through my mind that, he might come back out with just a walking stick. I was very grateful for the wheelchair. I was deposited in the chair and wheeled in.

At the reception desk, he started to tell them all about his little finger, that the week previous, he had dropped the ramp of the lorry on, they booked him in. This was his opportune moment. It was a bit of a mess, he just hadn't had time to go and get it checked out. I was forgotten about, until someone came in and complained about a car being dumped in the middle of the car park. Then, I was remembered! Alan trotted off to move the car and I was wheeled off to be put in a bay to be looked at. I was there a fair while, doctors and nurses kept coming and going. I could hear Alan walking about in the corridor outside, going on about his finger. Every time someone new came in to my cubicle, they asked if he was with me and could they get rid of him. What could I say?

His finger wasn't broken, so he was happy, I was well broke, so I wasn't happy. I had bent the seven inch titanium plate in my leg and they wanted to straighten it. They wanted to straighten it whilst I was still conscious. I was wheeled off to yet another room, where a group of medics came in to hold me down, whilst Dr number 1 would straighten the plate. BOLLOCKS to that, I turned in to a modern day version of The Exorcist, complete with revolving head. They knocked me out! They knocked me out again, to put an external fixation on my leg. My leg was bolted twice through the fibula, as it was in three bits, my ankle had a bolt going through it and my foot had two bolts going through it. Could my life get any worse. Again, yes it could. I came round in a private room, full of morphine, hallucinating that the walls were moving, I couldn't work out where the snoring noise was coming from. Well it couldn't be me, I was awake, or was I? It was coming from the ward next door, the wall was vibrating with the volume of it. Thank god I wasn't in the bed next to the culprit. Oh wait, I was, the walls were paper thin. Some one kill me now.

A few days later they let me out, just so they could have me back in a week later to pin, plate and plaster my leg. Finally, I was released like an animal back to the wild. But not before enduring Helen's version of driving a wheelchair round Swindon Hospital like the hounds of hell were after us. She was no Lewis Hamilton! Speed, on the straight, yes. Cornering, major fail! I didn't go far when I made it to those doors at the Hospital, it was winter, we were snowed and iced up in Lambourn. But, now I had a plaster on my leg, I could ride my own horse. Result!!!

It wasn't until the plaster was eventually taken off, that I realised what a mess they had made of my leg. The foot wasn't set straight, they had put more pins in my ankle. In time they started to come out through the skin on the side of my ankle. The plate they had put in to hold the fibula together, was rubbing everything it came in to contact with, namely a stirrup leather. Altogether, I had one seven inch plate with seven pins holding that in place, one three inch plate with three pins holding that one, three pins holding my foot on and another three pins screwed in to my ankle. Something had to go. The stirrup leather was rubbing my leg when I rode. Back I went to hospital, to get them to remove the three inch plate with it's pins, and the pins in my ankle. Yes, I do have to be a bit careful with my leg, but it's a lot better without all that metal inside it. The open wounds from the pins coming out through the skin, would have led to infection at some stage, and they were more painful than breaking my leg.

Thank goodness for Oaksey House in Lambourn, their rehab facility really is second to none. They got me walking again, yes I had to work at it, I walked miles on my crutches once the snow and ice had abated. It was a laugh at Oaksey, we were all riders, be it work riders, jockeys etc. We took the mickey out of each other and bolstered each other up. Some of the people who go there will never walk again, let alone sit on a horse. I was lucky.

39

Working for Alan was interesting to say the least. It was like working for an absent minded professor. I have never come across a man who was such a stickler for things being done a certain way. It was borderline obsession. As I said before, he worked very hard and loved his horses. The yard wasn't the best, but he made it work. The horses I looked after, lived right outside his front door.

These were the brick stables that would flood when it was wet. The stables were slightly below ground level on the road side, so the water from the road would seep in through the brickwork. A lot of places in Lambourn and the surrounding villages have no drains. Rainwater runs down the road till it finds a gateway, usually a field. The road between Compton and Long Hedge, is flat and regularly floods. When it's cold, there is frequently black ice on that stretch of road. Alan liked to use a certain type of bedding that soaked everything up, but we were only allowed to use two bales of bedding a week. In most stables the allowance is three bales of shavings a week. The theory behind the bedding we used, was that was was cost effective. It so wasn't! My horses were on wet bedding, Alan was forever on my back for throwing too much out. I kid you not, some mornings, the beds were that wet it looked like soup. I would end up dragging my muck bin across the yard to the trailer, because I just couldn't lift it.

Then, we had the performance of getting the bedding. He wouldn't have it delivered, he picked it up himself, in a horse trailer, might as well have put it in the lorry, but no. We had to stay behind one night a week, in order to unload the bedding into one of the stables where it was stored. The haylage the horses ate, was dropped off at the gate. We, the girls, would then manhandle the bales in to another spare stable. I swear by the time I left there, I was built like an Irish navvy. I had muscles in places I didn't know I had. I also had blisters on my backside from riding in his antiquated saddles, and that was despite using a seat saver.

We were often late finishing morning stables, but we still had to be back at 4pm no matter what. It didn't matter that some days I didn't leave till 1.30pm, if I was a minute late he would be at the gate looking at his watch. We often didn't leave till 6.30pm either. Yes we got paid overtime, but we needed to get away from the place, some days it just didn't happen. Weekends on, were a nightmare, Sunday morning especially. I was often still there at 11.30am, every other yard was usually finished between 9 and 10 am.

Apart from his constant falling out with Jan, and his complete disregard for time, he was okay for a boss. After I came off Flying Free, he was incredibly decent with me. It was a shame when he decided to pack in training. Alan returned to his old boss. He just didn't get the horses that could have changed his life.

40

LAMBOURN LIFE

It was while I was on crutches, doing my daily work out, that I got to see just how strange Lambourn can actually be. Whilst you are working in racing, you are permanently tired, and you don't really take notice of the eccentricities going on around you. It's par for the course.

One morning, I was walking my dog through a local housing estate, I was on a hill, looking down on the road that leads out of Lambourn. I noticed this pale figure running along the main road, hiding behind cars and going in to various gardens. It took a while for the penny to drop, that he was completely starkers. He was crouching down to hide behind bins, when a car approached, looked like he was taking a dump to be honest. Turned out, he was a new lad, just started at a stables in Kingston Lilse and this was his initiation ceremony. To be stripped bare, dropped off in Lambourn and to make own his way back to the yard. Poor lad had about three miles to go, running and ducking out of sight.

In the middle of Lambourn there is a crossroad, in the middle of the crossroad is a large round drain cover. That is not unusual, what is unusual is the amount of times the drain cover goes missing. Put that together, with a lack of decent street lights, it can become a problem. When I first moved to Lambourn, our own horses were kept out of the village at a place called Challow, heading towards Wantage. I was told to cut through a back lane to avoid driving down the hole. Good advice that was.

Later on, when our own horses moved to a farm up Maddle Road, life became a lot easier. When I broke my leg, I was having to drive through the strings in the mornings, instead of riding with the strings. That became an education. I was seeing things from a drivers point of view, and in a lot of cases it wasn't pretty. I could see why some drivers had no respect for horses on the road.

The worst case scenario was meeting the Green Gremlins. Stone me, they were the most ignorant bunch of cretins, I have ever had the misfortune to come across. Their yard was situated on the main road going in to Upper Lambourn. They just walked straight out on to the main road, it didn't matter what was on the road; it could be another string of horses, a single horse, car, or a lorry, they, the other road user were expected to move. The Green Gremlins, then wandered all over the road so nothing could get past them. Any vehicles, be it a car or lorry coming in the either direction, would have to stop completely at times, or be in danger of being hit by a horse. It was unbelievable. They wouldn't thank the other road users for being considerate towards them, it appeared to be completely beneath them. When, they had finally made it to the gallop, usually Fishers. The performance of watching them putting their jerks up, and checking their girths, was like watching a bunch of epileptic leprechauns.

Back then, not many yards rode out in Hi-Vis, so on the mornings it was dark, you really had to be on the look out for horses. The main clue was sparks coming from the horses shoes if they were travelling away from you, and if they were coming towards you, the headlights on the car would hopefully pick up the toe clips on the front shoes. That was providing that they had toe clips. More than once, I was told off for not seeing dark horses, on dark roads. The joy of Mandown Gallops in the winter months, it's a game of spot the horse, lets travel incognito, then blame everyone else, when the horse nearly gets hit by a car...

I once passed a horse painted as a Christmas jumper, again that was in the dark, it wasn't until I drew level, that I noticed half the horse was green. It was on it's way to a photo shoot for The Racing Post and was to be partnered with AP McCoy. I had given up being surprised by what I saw by this stage. Although I did laugh a lot at what I did see.

Monday mornings were my favourite mornings. Quite a lot of the lads were hung over, suffering the effects of a heavy weekend. It didn't matter if it was your weekend on or off, you were determined to enjoy it. I would pass riders sat on their bum in the middle of the road or just laying there, they had given up! I always called out 'okay?' And 'where's the horse?' Often, I had to get out of the car to either fetch a horse back to it's rider, put them back on board, or lead them on to the gallop, hoping that they were still on when they reached the end.

Then you got the 'Twitchers'. They were the drug takers. Racing is a hard game, some people turn to drugs, to help them keep them going and in some cases, to help them lose weight. They sit there on their horses, twitching and sniffing, with their eye balls out on stalks, or barely awake, but then again, that could also be the after effects of being up all night! And what they had taken!

A lot of the lads are gamblers, some spend all their wages in the bookies. Often, they put silly amounts on their own horses, in the hopes that there will be a big return. Then, they can revel in the prestige of looking after and riding a winning horse. They take a lot of pride in their horses.

41

THE IRISH

The saying 'the luck of the Irish' is spot on. The things they do and get away with is insane. They are a different breed, usually very good horsemen, combined with a good sense of humour. That's vital for seeing them through the scrapes they get themselves in to.

At one of the yards I worked at, two young Irish lads had just started working there. As it was their first morning, they were basically left to their own devices after they had ridden out. Well, these two found it hilarious when one of them fell over in the muck trailer, the other one joined him and there they were, rolling around in the shit and throwing it at one another, laughing their heads off. One of them went on to become a very good National Hunt jockey.

Then there was the unlucky trainer. My word he was unlucky, I don't think that the word unlucky, covered his training career. Doomed. That is a more accurate description. His tenacity was second to non. He moved in to his new rented premises to train, he must have thought his dreams had come true, the house was lovely. Unfortunately when he had the oil tank in the garden filled up, it turned out to have a massive leak and all the oil seeped away. Half his stables were unusable. He had a brood mare with a foal at foot. This foal was the devils work. It had 666 tattooed on it's forehead. It kicked him so hard in the balls one day, the lad he had working for him, had to drag him out of the stable because he couldn't walk. Then, no sooner had he recovered from that kicking, but it kicked him again, this time in the head. He was carted off to hospital and told not to ride. Next day he was riding out, complete with his head swathed in bandages, with his riding hat perched on top. His lad wouldn't ride with him, because everyone was laughing. Last I heard he had stopped training.

42

DARK SIDE

Every job has a dark side, Lambourn and horse racing is no exception. There is quite a high mortality rate, there is a drink, drug and gambling problem throughout racing. One of the yards in Lambourn lost two Indian lads, they committed suicide within three years of each other. Then there are the attempts that go by unnoticed, everyone is so busy, the cry for help can be missed.

Quite a few lads and lasses throughout racing suffer from Anorexia and Bulimia, they are under pressure in some yards to be at a certain weight or below it. I was lucky enough to never have a weight problem. I certainly don't agree with the public weighing of riders, that is just not on and can lead to serious health problems both mentally and physical.

There is a charity set up to help racing people, but from what I have seen, if you are not 'in' with the right people, then you are on your own. On two different occasions I have needed physio from Oaksey House, I had to pay despite being employed in racing full time and entitled to free care at Oaksey. The excuse every time was that I wasn't on the books. What a load of crap.

I hope that it improves with time. I wasn't the only one to be denied the help I was entitled to. Some help they were.

I had a girl living with me for a while, not the Scots girl, this one was from a small Cornish village. She started work at a small yard for a very nice trainer, unfortunately the other girls he employed weren't that nice. Libby, the girl who lived with me, started to see a young lad, who turned out to have a steady girlfriend back home in Ireland. The girlfriend rocked up in Lambourn, to keep an eye on her wayward boyfriend. She got a job in the local pub, then it all went well and truly sour. This lad told Libby the usual tripe of; I'm finishing with my girlfriend, you're the one I want and of course she believed him. In the mean time he was telling his girlfriend, that Libby wouldn't leave him alone.

His girlfriend made friends in the pub that she worked in, and in time told her friends there, that, her boyfriend was being chased by a young girl who worked at so and so's yard. The friends also worked at this yard, they put two and two together. Blaming Libby for everything.

Let the bitching begin......

Instead of asking out right what was going on, mind you, no one knew what was happening except the lad, and to be honest I don't think any one would have believed her. It quickly escalated and Libby couldn't see a way out, but to make an attempt on her own life.

I was coming through the front door one night, when I received a phone call from her to say that, she thought she had done a silly thing. Her voice didn't sound right, then she said that she had taken a load of tablets. Thankfully, she was upstairs on her bed. When I burst through her door, she was surrounded by empty pill packets. I called the emergency services and the person I talked to was brilliant, she talked me through what to do until the paramedics got there. The hardest part was getting Libby off the bed, in to the bathroom and sticking my fingers down her throat. The paramedics were there in five minutes, they worked with Libby and talked to her with no regard to time. Eventually, they bundled her in to the ambulance and took her to hospital.

That was the best thing they could have done. It frightened the crap out of her. Overnight, the girl who was in the same room as Libby went berserk, smashed the mirror on the vanity unit and tried to slash her wrists. The psychiatric ward she was placed in was a dreadful place. There was an armed policeman standing guard outside the ward, he was there to protect the nursing staff. You just don't realise what is going on in some peoples lives. It's really sad.

When I picked Libby up, and brought her home, she was more at peace with herself. Her boss came to see her, he was deeply shocked by what had happened. In time, Libby went back home to Cornwall. She didn't return to her work in racing, she got herself sorted out and is doing really well for herself. Racing is not for everyone.

There are good people and bad people working in racing. When someone starts a job in horse racing, the employers want reliability, good riders and good horsemanship skills. They tend not to be that fussed if someone has a criminal record, to be fair, it's not really an issue so long as the job gets done. But sometimes things are overlooked if the lad or lass in question, are good at their job. Excuses are sometimes made for certain behaviour, which should not be tolerated under any circumstances.

A new lad turned up for work at a local yard, which an ex jockey was training from. Everything seemed above board. He worked hard, was good with his horses and rode well. Then he took a shine to one of the stable lasses from another yard. He came across her in the pub, if I remember right she found him creepy and left the pub. This lad was there with a few mates from his new yard. The girl had to walk back home to the yard, she worked and lived on. She couldn't drive, her yard was about a mile or so away, along a country lane with no street lights. Her walk was usually safe, even though it was in the dark. When she was half way home, she was grabbed from behind. She never heard anyone behind her, she was quite on the ball when it came to walking home by herself. That was how crafty he was, he made sure that, she had no idea he was following, stalking her. He tried to get her on the ground, she fought back, being a stable lass, she was pretty strong and gave as good as she got.

The next day, she couldn't work, her face was very bruised, he had knocked her front teeth out. She knew my daughter and that I wasn't working because of my leg. She needed a lift to Wantage, to see a dentist, but because of the state of her face she wouldn't catch the bus, also she would have had to walk the full length of Maddle Road, where the jockey club gallops are. The riders would recognise her and ask what had happened to her.

I arrived to pick her up, I barely recognised her. She was a pretty girl, he really had gone to town on her. But he hadn't raped her, she had fought him off and he had run away, when he got nowhere with her. She knew who had attacked her. The police went to his yard to question everyone. They all said 'no, he wouldn't do a thing like that, it must have been someone else, she was lying'. What they didn't know, was that on the way back from the dentist in my car, we met his string coming down Maddle Road. When he clocked who was in the passenger seat he jumped off his horse and hid behind it, I mean proper hid, he was crouched so as not to be noticed. If that isn't a guilty party I don't know what is.

This girls life was made a misery by his pals, she was called a liar, there was not enough evidence to prosecute him, as his mates gave him an alibi. She couldn't even go for a quiet drink in any of the village pubs, without someone having a go at her. Eventually, this lad returned to Ireland. Not long after he had started work on a yard, he attacked another girl who he worked with. This time the police managed to do him for that attack, turns out he had done it before and got away with it. He got put away for a time. There were a few shamefaced lads in Lambourn after that.

43

BITS AND BOBS

When, I was finally able to start work again, I didn't want to go back in to racing, so I worked at various yards as a groom and yard person. I had been warned that if I broke my leg again, then I would probably lose it. Also, it had taken a year for the bones to knit together, so I really didn't want to risk it.

I had two or three part time jobs on the go. One was with a showjumper who was never around, despite her owners paying her a hefty fee to ride and train their horses. She did however believe in turning her horses out, so that redeemed her in my book, although she never had any money left at the end of the month to pay me, so I left.

Another employer was an American, who had rode in the Olympics for their eventing team. I couldn't get over her tack. She had the most beautiful saddles and bridles. She rode exceptionally well. I would have killed to be able to ride like she could, but she had lost her nerve. She always rode in the school, never went for a hack. My job, was to bolster her confidence whilst she was on board, she constantly questioned her ability to leave the ground, going over a jump. Her position was always perfect and I never saw her approach a jump wrong.

She had a brood mare who had terrible thrush, that's a fungal infection in the foot. Her way to treat it, was to soak pieces of cotton wool in water, push the cotton wool in to the infected areas with a farriers nail to clean away the muck. It didn't work, but that was how she wanted it done. She bred a gelding, who was two years old at the time I was there from this mare, who although well grown was absolutely shocking behind. Nothing was right about his quarters or his back legs. He looked like he had had a fight with a spin dryer and lost. He was going to be her next top horse. I didn't stay there long, lovely lady, but she did my head in.

Next up, were a couple of part time jobs with racehorses, but on the ground. There were only four or five horses in each yard to look after in the morning. One of them was for a man who did not have a good reputation in Lambourn, but his horses needed looking after, and I am one of those people who like to make my own mind up about people. Gossip can be so malicious and damaging especially if it's not true. It was true in this case!!! Ah well, you live and learn.

A friend of mine was training in East Lambrook, not far from Lambourn and they needed help with their horses. When I first came to Lambourn, I used to ride out for her and her partner after morning stables, as they were quite a distance away from Lambourn, no one wanted to go that far. They always paid really well and the horses were easy. When they moved yards to be nearer to the gallops at Lambourn, I was asked to help out in the mornings, as I didn't want to do full time, it worked well for us. They wanted me to ride out, but my leg was still healing and as time went by, I came to realise that I was fed up with riding with people who said that they could ride. I often ended up riding their horses at the same time as my own. Telling or suggesting to them, a way to ride the horse they were sat on, as they were incapable of riding it themselves. Harsh I know, but every decent rider will tell you the same thing.

I never went back to riding out professionally, I rode occasionally but that was it, I had my own horse to ride and I was content with that. My mare kept me sane over the years that I rode out for other people.

44

THE TRAINER ON THE HILL

There aren't many women trainers in racing, although there are more now, than when I first started in racing. I think they have more to prove as they are in a male dominated profession. People are watching and judging, waiting for them to fail, even before they have got a horse anywhere near a race track. Personally, I don't think it should matter as long as, the horses are looked after and trained properly.

Sue could get her horses fit, she trained them as eventers which worked for her. She had between ten to fifteen horses in training whilst I was working for her. Unfortunately, she didn't have the winners, that maybe she could have had. Maybe she wasn't picking the right races, for the right horses. Sue had one or two good horses who she thought the world of, she really appreciated having them in her yard. One of these was going to be sold to go to America to go steeplechasing. Rather a lot of money was being bandied around, but the horse ended up staying in this country.

The other successful horse she had, was consistently placed. He was a lovely character and always tried his hardest. I hope he was retired to enjoy a life out of racing, he certainly deserved it.

What I did like about Sue was that, she would leave no stone unturned, whilst trying to find a way to ride her horses to the best of their ability. She wasn't scared of calling the vet to check that everything was as good as it could be. She regularly had a chiropractor out to check her horses and herself. I hated having to go in to her house to ask her something, whilst he was in the house treating her, the noises that would come out of the living room were something else. It sounded like they were practising BDSM. Obviously they weren't as both were in happy relationships with other people.

She was open to all sorts of therapies, she tried Bach Remedies, Crystal Healing, you name it, she tried it. She expected her staff to learn, to improve themselves, but then, for some unknown reason, she would slap them back down again. Her chiropractor had developed a machine to help the horses that he treated. When he found out that I was training as an equine massage therapist, he was quite keen for me to buy one of his machines and treat the horses he sent my way. Of course, when Sue got wind of this, I was elbowed out of the way so that she could do it. Funny thing was, when I walked away, it wasn't what I really wanted to do, she lost interest in that venture.

Her head lad, at the time that I was there, was only eighteen years old. I remember her asking me before I started, if I would have a problem working under a young lad, that's come out wrong!! He would be my superior, the short answer is no. So long as he knows his job and isn't arrogant, I have no problem with that. Turned out we got on fine.

Sue found it difficult at times to get people to come and ride out for her, a lot of this was down to her forthright nature. Being straight wasn't a problem, it was the nit picking and the volume of the delivery that ticked people off. I became convinced that she had missed her calling, instead of being a racehorse trainer, she could have done a sterling job as a fog horn on Berry Head in Brixham. I could hear her yelling at her staff on the gallop and all the way back to the yard. In fact, I would recite it word for word when they came back. More than once she reduced the girls to tears over something trivial. Sue allowed one of the girls to pull one of the horses manes. Sue didn't notice how bad it was until they were half way to the gallop. The volume of 'Holly!!!! What the f*** have you done to this horses mane? If you can't pull a mane don't do it!' Echoed round the valley. The mood was immense, when the riders came back. To be fair the mane was a mess, it took months to grow out.

Sue had a small band of merry men, who would come and ride out for her for a few weeks, until they went deaf through her shouting or got fed up with being put down. They would then disappear for a time and turn up again at a later date, I presume when their hearing had returned to normal. One was an ex jockey who couldn't drive, I had to pick him up in the village as I drove through every morning. I never got over the fact that he couldn't drive, I mean how did he get to race meetings? He must have cadged a lift everywhere. Bet that went down well. His nerve wasn't brilliant, he would ask me to lunge his horses for twenty minutes or more before he would sit on them. But he only asked me when Sue was out of the way, eventually she caught me lunging one of the horses he was supposed to be sat on, she got rid of him. Her horses were easy to do, they were fed correctly for the work that they did.

I lunged her horses in the field opposite her yard. It was right on top of a hill, the wind would blow a gale up there. When it rained in Lambourn, I got pelted with hail the size of golf balls. It was usual to use almost the entire field to lunge in, the wind would launch the horse and myself all over the place. What was a simple job in other yards, was a feat in endurance, trying to stay in one place and not to take off.

The yard didn't have a horse walker, so the head lad and myself walked the horses that needed walking, in hand. This was okay until we met the neighbouring trainers string out for exercise. Then it got a little interesting, with us turning for home rather quickly. We would get a bollocking for returning home early. My answer to that was 'do it yourself then, I don't get paid enough to be turned in to a human kite'.

45

STUD DUTIES

Sue had a brood mare who, she had bred some decent horses from. As I could drive the lorry, I got sent to pick this mare up from the stud she was at. I had a lovely peaceful drive to an area in Staffordshire I had never been to before. Once on the lorry, the mare yelled all the way home, a bit like her owner! When we arrived home, the ramp went down on the lorry, the disgust on this mares face when she realised where she was, well, she made me laugh. I think it was fair to say she didn't like her home. Unfortunately she wasn't in foal, so a few weeks later she was loaded back on the lorry and taken back. She bounced up that ramp all happy. What she didn't know was that it was a flying visit, she was coming back the same day. I was to wait whilst she was covered by the stallion. Travelling there I had a happy quiet horse on board. Until, we drew near the stud then she started to call out. I'm sure she was saying 'Hi guys, I'm back!' The ramp went down at the stud, she surveyed her surroundings and marched down the ramp like a queen.

The couple who owned the stallion were quite old. The mare was taken by the lady, and the man went to get the stallion. He was a lovely horse, he has sired a lot of National Hunt horses, sadly he's not alive any more. As the mare was going to be covered in hand, I was invited to go and watch! Lucky me! Not what I was expecting. I didn't particularly want to watch, I was quite happy to sit in the lorry until the deed was done.

I trundled along behind, until we came to a path that opened up to a circular area. The mare had her hind feet hobbled, so that she couldn't kick her suitor. No fear of that I might add, she was well up for it! The dirty minx, I'm standing there waiting for a younger person to come along and hold the stallion, but no, there was no younger person. I had this fleeting vision of it all going wrong. The man looked very fragile next to this rampant stallion. Then, the stallion was on the mare, he couldn't find the right hole, so the man gets hold of the stallions 'bits' to help. The stallion was outraged, he broke free. That's when I legged it back to the lorry, locking myself in the cab, I'm sat there waiting for an irate stallion to come round the corner, when it dawned on me that I was sat in a fibreglass cab. Not much protection there. I got out and locked myself in a stable. I was an absolute wetty.

No stallion arrived, thank god. The couple arrived with my mare all smiles, the covering was complete! The mare then wouldn't load, she wanted to stay with her husband. She went on eventually, she bawled all the way home, then sulked when she was put in a stable. She was found to not be in foal again. It was getting a bit late in the season for covering, so Sue waited until the following year, then sent the mare back to her usual husband. The mare caught straight away. That's horses for you! That was my one and only foray in to breeding/stud work. It's not for me.

46

OLD YARDS

There are a lot of very old training yards in and around Lambourn. Some are steeped in history and are very quaint. Others need pulling down. Sue's yard was in the latter. Her horses were never really well despite her best efforts. She blamed the stables themselves, she used wood pellets for bedding, which were delivered from Liverpool, a pallet at a time. We would open up the bags, stick the hose pipe in and fill the bag up with water, this was so that the pellets inside could swell up, then they would be scattered in the stables. No horse is going to stay well living and sleeping on permanently wet bedding, especially in the cold weather. Their rugs were covered in wet sloppy shit. Nothing was ever dry in the stables. In winter it was baltic for the horses. Quite a few horses would get abscess'. What can you expect, when the horses were standing in a wet bed for twenty three hours a day, then stepping out on to a surface made of hardcore.

We were forever clipping horses, Sue didn't get that the horses were cold because of the bedding she used, it made everything damp. She was always buying duvets to put under their rugs to keep them warm. When the horses laid down, their rugs and duvets got wet from the bedding. So their coats grew back quickly to keep them warm.

The water for the yard was run from a pump. There were a couple of neighbours who had complained about the noise from the pump in the morning. Therefore, we were not allowed to give the horses fresh water first thing. Horses going out first lot, couldn't have a drink unless it was dirty, when they returned from exercise. Fresh clean water should be available at all times. But hey ho, the neighbours knew best! Sue was frightened of upsetting the neighbours, if she lost her stables then not only did she lose her income, but her home as well. Sue's house was on the yard.

Sue's partner built her some extra stables out of breeze blocks, the one on the end kept falling down. Then, there were the wooden stables out the back. They also needed to be condemned, my biggest fear, was that they would fall down whilst I was on the yard by myself and there were horses in them. Again the water supply to these stables was iffy. Going back to the original stabling, it was an L shaped yard of well built, brick stables. The doors were something else, they were rotten through and through, some of the wood was infected with ringworm. Once you get the dreaded ringworm in the wood of stables, the horses that live in those stables will nearly always have ringworm at some time.

The mare that lived in the ringworm stable was plastered in the stuff, nothing we treated it with worked. We tried all the usual, the shampoos, the creams, potions and lotions, the veterinary prescribed treatments, everything was tried. In fact it got worse, the more we tried to get rid of the ringworm, the worse it got.

The owners of this mare were old school, when they saw her, instead of being furious at the state of their mare they suggested we use, used engine oil. What the hell? We had nothing to lose. We rounded up all the used oil we could find and applied it diligently everyday. It worked!! When she was finally healed, she went back home to her owners, we couldn't put anything else in the stable as the wood was clearly infected.

Our feed shed had an epic door on it, most of the time it hung there on one hinge. Eventually it fell off, leaving the feed at the mercy of the biggest rats I have ever seen. The saying 'rats as big as cats' was an understatement. Sue got two feral cats, a mother and a daughter from Cats Protection. War had been declared on the rat problem. After their mandatory stay in one of the stables for a couple of weeks, to get them used to their surroundings, we left both the doors open so that they could come out in their own time. They came out alright, they took one look at the size of the rats, and promptly jumped ship to the neighbouring farm, they didn't come back. We never saw them again. Bit ungrateful, I thought.

47

LEMMY

Lemmy was a horse who arrived from Ireland, late, one cold winters night. It was blowing a gale, again. He had had the journey from hell by all accounts. The ferry crossing had been rough. Lemmy practically fell off the lorry, when he finally ended his journey. He was exhausted. Sue put him in one of the biggest boxes, not the ringworm one, I might add, and let him recover for a few days. He was left to get his bearings, he didn't exactly look poor, but he didn't look right either. He the look of a horse who had been trained hard. He had gone in on himself. The lights were on, but no one was at home. It took a long, long time to get him to come out of himself.

When he was started back in work, it was as though something was missing. Sue went through everything with a fine tooth comb. Non of the bloods taken, showed what was wrong, he was given all sorts of treatments, as well as vitamins and minerals to try to make him well. He wasn't worked hard. He was turned out in the field most days. In the end out of desperation, Sue had heard of a man who lived in the village, who did treatments for equine allergies. She booked him to come and treat Lemmy.

I have to admit that at first we did poo hoo this treatment, not because it was Homeopathic, but because of how it was going to be administered. But Sue was always open to try anything if it helped her horses.

This man arrived at the yard with what can only be described, as one of those trays that are hung round the neck, like he was going to sell ice creams. In this were a selection of glass phials with all sorts of minerals in them. We were intrigued! Sue had decided that whilst he was there, he would see two other horses, as well as Lemmy. And the ideal person to help him with this was Moi! Off we went to the first stable, I was to hold the horse whilst he rummaged around in his ice cream tray. He chose his phials, one in each hand and held his arms out, elbows bent at right angles from his body. My job, and I kid you not, was to push his arms down as hard as I could, as he pushed back. He kept changing the phials until there was no resistance, between him and myself, which told him he had found the right mixture of minerals for that horses' problems. All the while I was pushing his arms down, he was staring intently at me, I was waiting for him to start chanting or the very least go 'Ommm'. But no, I amazed myself with my self control, all I wanted to do was laugh, I know that sounds bad, I couldn't look at him. I got around the giggling, by having a chuckle in between horses. When we got to Lemmy, I just knew I was going to be stuck in there for an age, pushing his arms down and going 'Ommm' in my head. Eventually we were finished, I was knackered, it was easier to ride a strong horse than to help that man.

He went off to talk to Sue, telling her that the remedies for each of the horses' he had seen, would be made up and delivered in a couple of days. Two days later he reappeared with his potions.

Non of us were that hopeful that it would work on Lemmy, but we followed the man's instructions to the letter. By the end of the week, Lemmy was starting to improve. The other two horses improved as well, but not like Lemmy. He came on in leaps and bounds, when his potion came to an end, Sue ordered some more. I do believe in Homeopathic treatments, but I didn't believe in the arm thing. Either way it worked for Lemmy.

48

HUNTING

Sue's head lad, Ben, wanted to ride in Point to Points, the idea being that he would get enough rides under his belt, then move on to riding in National Hunt races. The only problem was that, Sue would provide a horse for Ben to ride both, out hunting and pointing, but he couldn't drive the lorry and she was not prepared to find a driver for him, so I drove him. I found out that she would provide horses for her staff to take to places, but then not allow them to use her lorry or allow any one to groom for them. It was rather like giving with one hand and taking with the other, bit unfair I thought.

For a horse to qualify to take part in a Point to Point, they have to go hunting four times, to get their card stamped to prove that they have actually gone hunting, not just turned up, got the card stamped and then gone back home. It does happen. Ben I spent that winter hunting on most Sunday's, he learnt a lot from that and he did progress to having a few rides. Ben worked his backside off for Sue, she taught him a lot, but she could be very unfair to him at times, He eventually left Sue to work in a large National Hunt yard in Cheltenham, I think he did quite well, he certainly got a lot more rides, but then they had more horses.

Sue could be plain mean to all members of her staff, then she would wonder why they upped and left. It was nothing to work both Christmas and New Year, as she would change her mind at the last minute about which one she was going to work or not in her case. Her excuse was that she had a family, so did everyone else. You can't just abandon horses in stables because it's the festive period, there were only three members of staff including Sue, to look after those horses. The quicker you got done, the quicker you got home in theory. She would leave a great big list of things to be done on Christmas Day, jobs that really didn't need doing. It was just Sue being a cow.

Ben's rides in pointing were on a horse that Sue had been training for quite sometime. He was owned by the lady who owned Sue's yard. He was a schoolmaster with a mind of his own. Ideal to teach a young jockey the ropes.

She encouraged riders to get their licence out, but it was always a double edged sword. I know of one rider who on the day of her first race ride in pointing, actually got the lorry, but then had to lead her horse up herself, saddle it, weigh herself out and in, untack after the race, then drive herself and the horse home. Good job she didn't come off and end up in hospital.

Sue was a great one for 'doing the talk' but not that great at 'doing the walk'. I saw her on a racing program a while back, she was waxing lyrical about the pay and conditions in racing, about the fact that racing staff usually only have three full days a month off. I wanted to phone in and remind her that whilst I worked for her, I worked both Christmas and New Year, the head lad and myself didn't get a day off for six weeks. I heard more than once, that if she employed someone and provided their accommodation, she charged full whack. Most yards subsidise their employees living arrangements by taking a nominal sum from their wages each week or month, if they live in accommodation provided by their employer. Sue's employees had to plan very carefully when they gave her their notice. They were often thrown out of the flat as soon as they gave their notice, and told that their job was finished. When I gave her my notice, she told me not to work the notice out, I was done. That suited me!

49

WOODSIDE

I vividly remember the first day I drove up to Woodside. I had spoken to the boss Bertie, on the phone and he sent me up to Woodside to meet the head lad. I turned off the main road and was greeted with two large signs. The one on the left, said Woodside Stud, the one on the right, said Woodside. I made my way in the car down a long drive. Post and rail fencing, on the right hand side ran the length of the drive. A tall hedge was on the left, which was broken up by wooden gates, one for each paddock, all the gates on both sides of the drive, had the name of a past equine inmate on a plaque, as a tribute to the successful Thoroughbred horses who had lived at Woodside. I was in paradise. This truly was the stuff dreams are made of. If you were horsey that was.

I arrived at a pair of white gates, they magically opened as I drew near. I had never come across electric gates before. In time they were to become the bane of my life. On passing through them, there was a small cul de sac with six houses on my right and a large cream house on my left. Beyond that on the right were, two L shaped stable yards made up of green painted wooden boxes. I was to follow the road round to the left, park up, go through more white gates, then into the red brick yard on the right. The yard was practically empty. It held twenty nine stables, a vet box, a solarium and a full size tack room. Across the courtyard I had walked through, on the left there was another yard which also held twenty nine boxes, and a full size tack room. And in time to come a salt room was added to this yard.

I found the head lad in a stable bandaging a horse. There were only fourteen horses in training there at the time. I joined the team the following Monday. There were only four of us working on the yard. Tina, the travelling head lass, Louise, the stable lass, Sam, the head lad and of course me, the newly employed yard person. I had no wish to ride out any more so this suited me. The down side was that we used muck sacks, clambered up steep steps at the side of the trailer, with said muck sack weighing a ton on your back and depositing the muck in the trailer. Then you congratulated yourself that a) you stayed upright and b) you didn't fall backwards down the steps, ending up in the muck sack itself. I really enjoyed the early days there. I loved working for Bertie and his wife Patsy, they were old school and I like that. We were all employed by a large company with horses and studs all over the world.

As winter approached seven horses were sent to the sales, to make way for yearlings that were going to come in for breaking and training. That first winter we spent twiddling our thumbs and looking at each other. The yard was pristine and so were the horses. You could have eaten your dinner off the floors and the horses. When the fourteen yearlings arrived, we then had twenty one horses. The number of horses more or less doubled each year, eventually all the yards on the estate reached full capacity of a hundred horses.

Woodside has it's own gallops both grass and artificial. When I first started there was only one gallop/groundsman. It's a big place so I think he had his work cut out for him. Bertie's son John, was a trainer in his own right, when he moved his training yard up to Woodside, we gained another groundsman.

John was a lovely man, he let me borrow his lorry a few times, but he wouldn't let me pay him for the use of it, so I always made sure I put extra diesel in the tank and took a couple of bottles of red wine to him, to say thank you. He stayed there until his untimely death through illness. After his death, Bertie took over training his sons horses until the yard was closed down. Then we inherited a secretary as we didn't have one, the head lads wife was our secretary along side her day job.

50

I really liked Bertie and Patsy I loved working for them. They knew their horses and they knew their staff. Every single morning they went round the yard saying hello to every member of staff. You were made to feel that you were part of a family. They created a happy atmosphere for the horses to live and work in, I think that could be part of the reason he was such a successful trainer. He knew how to get his horses fit. When I moved to Lambourn I thought that this was a given. I came to realise that some of the fittest horses I had ever ridden were my own and at Barbers. Trainers were often left scratching their heads wondering why they couldn't get their horses to win races. They need to be fit. BertieFor the last sixteen years years or so, I have had a blast. regularly produced winners at Woodside, as had the trainers who had been there before him.

If a horse went wrong, which to be fair didn't happen that often with Bertie training it, then that horse was given proper time to recover and for his body to heal. The horses on box rest weren't ignored, the people who looked after them were asked plenty of questions about their welfare; how were they behaving, were they getting any better, moving round the box any easier. Would it be better to send them back home to the stud to recover, all this was taken in to account. Bertie listened to his head lad, heeded his advice and took on board what his riders had to say.

He also dealt with feedback from when horses went racing, be it human or horse. He didn't bury his head in the sand hoping the problem would go away. He dealt with it head on. We had a lad who was good at his job, but was his own worse enemy. Adam liked to gamble and seemed to be very good at it. He showed me his betting account one day, I nearly fell through the floor. He was a bit hands on and went for the apprentice one day. He had this eight stone lad pinned up against the wall by his throat, The apprentice had been running his mouth off and he'd been found out. Adam had also turned up worse for wear, to lead a horse up at a race meeting. He had to go, but the company had to follow certain guidelines, our new secretary was a stickler for rules. The longer it took to remove this lad legally, the more Bertie disliked him.

Bertie and Patsy liked to look after their staff, there were a number of empty houses on the estate. The house I was living in, in the village was going to be sold, so I was given a house to live in. I had always been wary of living on site, where my place of work was. Sue Major confirmed that to me, but this was different. There was a load of paperwork to protect both myself and the company. The company was very generous to it's employees. I had a three bedroom house with a large garden, all I paid for was the electric and the oil for heating. The company paid for the water and council tax. My daughter was living with me at the time, so this worked out really well.

The downside if you could call it that, was fighting to get out first thing in the morning to do our horses. The electric gates had a mind of their own. If they decided that they were not going to open, I was stuffed. So I started to leave my car on the other side of the gates. As I left the house so early, I often didn't bother to open the downstairs curtains. This would infuriate Bertie, he would say to me to open them, as it looked liked someone had died. Made me laugh that did.

As Bertie loved his garden, he ordered some hanging baskets for the yards. They were beautiful and very big. When Bertie retired and Oliver took over the following summer, Oliver ordered some hanging baskets for the ards. Talk about small, they got lost on the hangers.

51

EX JOCKEYS

There are quite a few ex jockeys floating around. Some finish their careers because of injury; they have lost their nerve, can't get enough rides to make a living out of the game, they can't keep their weight down or they have plain had enough. Sometimes they retrain with JETS, which is a charity for ex jockeys so that they can go on to have a different career. Some become trainers in their own right, some are very good and some not. There are those who can't quite rid themselves of the racing obsession and ride out for various trainers. As you can earn more money as a freelance work rider than a full time member of staff, this is quite tempting.

Nigel was taken on as a full time stable lad. He needed a job and a roof over his head. He had been a very good jockey, he had ridden all over the world. We weren't sure what to expect and he was probably feeling the same. He started off grand, he mucked in with the rest of us. We now had wheelbarrows. Yippee! The company had finally been dragged in to the twenty first century. The muck sacks were obsolete.

Nigel had a drink problem, I don't think anyone realised just how bad it was, until it started to be brought on to the yard. He would come in to work first thing in the morning drunk. There were a couple of times he appeared looking like he had been in a fight. Technically he had. He had been trying to ride his moped back to the yard after a night out and fallen off a number of times as he was so drunk. How he didn't get hit by a car on Hungerford Hill was anyone's guess.

Evening stables could be pure entertainment. He would stagger round doing his horses, merrily leaving his doors open, somehow nothing escaped. I think that was down to pure luck. One afternoon I walked in to the two year old yard to find Paul crying with laughter, when he could finally speak, he said that Nigel had been pushing his wheelbarrow up the ramp in to the trailer, managed to tip it up to empty it, but then it had all gone wrong and somehow the wheelbarrow ended up on top of him, with him inside it. Of course he couldn't get out. We used those massive wheelbarrows that can can carry two or three bales of hay. Paul had to rescue him.

Things got dangerous when he turned up for work at 6.45am, he was not just drunk, but absolutely hammered. He was rarely late no matter what state he was in. And to be fair he nearly always did his work. He was legged up on to a colt and pulled out with the string at 7.30am. By 7.45am all hell had broke loose, Nigel had come off his colt, his colt had made a bee line for Paul's colt, Paul couldn't get out of the way, he couldn't get off and he was wearing two metal earrings. Nigel's colt was trying to shag Paul's colt. The only thing Paul could do was to make a run back to the yard for help.

I was hearing my name being yelled but couldn't work out where it was coming from until, Paul appeared in the entrance to the three year old yard, still yelling with Nigel's colt trying it's best to mount Paul's colt. Thank god one of the riders had been jocked off and was on the yard with me, we had to get in between the colts, separate them and by this time they were having a proper ding dong with each other. Paul managed to jump off safely. It was managed quickly, surprisingly Paul wasn't hurt, the two colts were cut up and banged about a bit, but it could have been so much worse. Nigel was banned from riding for a bit.

As Nigel wasn't allowed to ride out until he got his act together, I was lumbered with him on the yard. Fortunately we got on well together and he did pull his weight. He never made silly excuses for being drunk, he said it as it was and I liked him for that. Then he started to disappear when first lot pulled out and wouldn't come back till just before they were due back in. As Woodside is quite a big place, I would come back up to the top yards from the bottom yards to find his stables not mucked out and horses arriving back in. Horses do not come back from exercise to go back in to dirty stables, everything is fresh or it should be. I don't really know why he bothered to come back on the yard when first lot were due back, as we went for breakfast straight after.

Something had to be done when we came back from breakfast one day, after second lot had pulled out. Nigel had gone in to a colts stable to muck it out, he hadn't got as far as pulling the wheelbarrow in the doorway, when he left the door wide open and sat down between the colts front legs. He could barely move.

It was a real shame as he was a really nice man, we all liked him, but he was ill. Whilst he was on the yard with me, we used to talk about all sorts of things. One of the things he wanted to do was to be a gardener. I heard he went back home to Yorkshire, I hope he's happy and doing some gardening.

Percy was one of three Brazilian brothers who came to work with us, they were all ex jockeys. After a time two of the brothers left for another yard in Lambourn, Percy remained at Woodside. He was a quiet man until he got stuck in to the booze on a Friday afternoon, then all hell could break loose. He would leave his equipment for evening stables down at the six box area. One afternoon, someone had taken his fork and left a broken one. Instead of going to find another fork he attempted to muck his stables out with the broken one, which of course he couldn't do. He lost his rag, big time and started to scream that he was going to kill all of us. As he was drunk we were not too sure which way this would go, so he was sent home in disgrace to the hostel, where he lived with some of the other members of staff. The following morning he appeared in his usual quiet manner and rather shame faced.

The hostel had a number of single bedrooms, with a kitchen and lounge area, it was mainly used by the guys. When the French man moved in, the hostel turned in to a war zone. The French man would wind Percy up to the point that he would go for him with a knife. They both hated each other, but couldn't leave each other alone, Friday nights consisted of the French man being chased round the pool table with threats of being killed. More than once the Assistant Trainer had to go in and break them up.

The French man had moved over from France with his partner and their little girl, but unfortunately the relationship floundered and so he ended up in the hostel. He was very good at his job and absolutely detested sloppiness. He didn't like us very much either to be honest. Every single one of us copped it from him at sometime. I couldn't always make out what he was saying until he got to the 'you are zhit' moment, which he said a lot. He worked incredibly hard even when he had done his back in, he was in agony, but he still came in to work on the yard, he couldn't ride out, but couldn't bear to be at home doing nothing. I think he missed calling us all 'zhit'.

52

YARDIES

As we got more horses, we got more riders and another yardy turned up. We got quite excited about this, well I did. I was the only yardy in a yard of about thirty horses by that stage. The lads mucked out three horses each before pulling out, but I had to get all the bales of shavings and bales of hay round from the barns to the yards, as well as my own horses to muck out, which could be as many as fourteen plus, then there were the yards to brush. Luckily we had a blower and later on a yard hoover which lasted all of five minutes. Rumour had it our new yardy had been a head lad for a very successful yard over in Ireland. Since coming back to the main land he had worked for a couple of trainers here in Lambourn.

Monday morning came round, and the new yard person appeared. He was over six foot tall and borderline six foot round the middle. I didn't care as I needed help. Phil was as loud as he was tall, he had a broad Lancashire accent. He was ex army and got stuck in to everything. We worked well together until he lost his rag, then it was like Jekyll and Hyde, there was no warning that the explosion was imminent, it just happened. I made things worse on occasions, I would not be intimidated by him and would often shout back, eyeballing his chest as he towered over me.

He was another one who broke his fork in a temper, because he couldn't actually kill the person who had irked him. Admittedly the person in question would annoy Phil just to watch the fun and games erupt. Then the comments of 'you killed a bale of shavings, well done.' 'What's that fork ever done to you?' Really didn't go down well at all. Phil would be purple with rage, screaming from inside the stable that he was going to snap Tim in half. Tim always replied, 'you've got to catch me first, you fat b******'. Lovely, another epic morning on the yard.....

When it was just Phil and myself on the yards we got things done in quick time. Later on when more yard people were employed, we realised just how slow they worked. Phil turned out not to have any horse experience, apart from mucking out and bossing other staff around. He'd never sat on a horse, he had raced greyhounds back in Ireland and was very successful by all accounts, then he switched to horses. Thoroughbred's are sensitive creatures and can pick up straight away if someone is nervous or bolshy round them. Colts are particularly adept at this. They clock you straight away.

We would start mucking out in one yard, working our way round the empty boxes, then start on the ones with occupants. One colt rarely went out first lot, so he was on our list. He was rose grey in colour and sired by Zebedee, he was one of those who either liked you or hated you. There was nothing in between. Phil chose, and I use that word, chose, to muck this colt out, I had already said that I would do him, but Phil thought he was doing the right thing. Oh, how he lived to regret that one.

No sooner had he opened the door and shut himself in, than the colt went for him, poor Phil stood no chance in trying to get the head collar on. I heard cries of 'help, help', when I looked up. Phil had his head out through the anti weave grill, his arms and shoulders were still in the stable, he couldn't get to the bolt. Behind him, I could see teeth gnashing and a grey tail going round in the stable like a flag, I hot footed it over there to get Phil out before he was killed. He wasn't physically harmed, but his pride took a hell of a knock. I did the colt from then on. In fact he became one of the horses I looked after. He was quite a guarded horse, when you got over that, he was grand.

Phil became our feed man, how, I don't know, as he had no knowledge of horses, but this became the norm at Woodside after Bertie retired. He was having trouble walking, and the continuous lifting and throwing of bales round took it's toll on him. Phil would muck out five horses first thing, then retire to the feed room for the rest of the morning only coming out for a fag when the need arose, unless the shout went up 'loose one' from either the indoor ride or incoming from the gallop, then he was expected to make an appearance in some attempt to stop the horse before any damage could be done.

On the morning that is forever etched in my memory, I was working down the bottom yards with Bryan. We were on our way back up to the top, to start filling up the trolleys to take hay to the stables in the bottom yards, when the call went up 'loose one'. We immediately started in the direction of the indoor ride as there were no other places for horses to be loose, the gate to the gallop was shut. Bryan clocked Phil come hurrying out of the feed room, heading for the ride.

'Come on' I said 'we had best get up there'.

'Hang fire a minute Bill', Bryan said as he held my arm back. 'Let's just see how this unfolds'.

'But he'll get hurt' I said.

To which Bryan replied 'with a bit of luck'. And there was I thinking that they were friends! They were friends, but it was Bryan's sense of humour.

The horse had dumped his pilot and was merrily cantering past all the other horses in the ride. The doors were wide open, if the horse came flying out of the ride there was a danger that he would slip and fall on the concrete. There was only one person on the door and she had no chance of stopping the colt. Enter our hero Phil. As he marched across the concrete yard to the ride, we could hear his voice saying 'I'll catch 'orse'. So we let him catch 'orse and laughed a hell of a lot afterwards.

He walked in to the middle of the ride, put his arms out and stood there waiting for the horse to come round again. I was impressed that he was facing the right way. I think in all seriousness that Phil thought that his size would bring the horse to a halt. But no! It ran over the top of him and carried on. He lay there like a beached whale. Fortunately he wasn't hurt, again. At what point did he think that was going to work? Bless him for trying.

We had a number of foreign yard people start, on the whole they were great. You will always get the odd one, who tries to pull a fast one and do as little as possible, but we also had English people do the same. What I couldn't abide was some, not all, of the new yard people getting a few horses to muck out, put on the walker and then refusing to help out on our other yards.

We had two yard people on the two top yards, they had eight horses each to muck out. When they had finished, instead of helping other people and making a start on filling up the hay stables, I used to find them reclining, that is the correct word, as they were horizontal on the hay bales, having a rest. The lads down the bottom yards were doing up to sixteen stables a morning, I was doing the same, but I floated round the yards mucking out what needed doing and so on. I got an app on my phone to work out how many miles I was covering each day. It was eleven miles, I knew Woodside was a large place but to walk that many miles each and every day was ridiculous. Especially as I was chasing up lazy so and so's, who would pull the racist crap when they were asked why they wouldn't help out in the other yards.

53

Bryan was a godsend. Yes he could be a gobshite, but then who couldn't? We got on really well, we had the same sick sense of humour. He loved his horses and always did them up to the best of his ability. On his first day he knew who I was, but I didn't know him. What I liked straight away was that I didn't have to stand over him to make sure he was working. Once he had sussed out where his horses were, he was away.

As soon as he could, he went down to the bottom yards to work. They became 'his yards'. I didn't blame him, there were too many prima donas in the top yards. He preferred to muck out twice as many boxes just to get out of the way. The only downside was that all the work boards were in the main older horse yard. We had a board for who was mucking out what horse, who was riding what horse, who was walking, trotting, cantering and working (galloping).Which horses were on box rest, which horses were on the treadmill. Which horses were going to the vets, who was going with the horse to the vets. Which horses were going in the spa, the walker, the salt room, who was going racing and who was scratching their backsides. A board for every eventuality! Thank god for phones that take photos.

I have to admit that as soon as I could, I would escape from the top yards. Sad, I know! Bryan made the place more bearable, he did make me laugh. It was Bryan who got me through the shit that was going on in my personal life. He listened without judgement and then made me laugh. He was an ex jockey, so he had been around a while, he had seen most things and like me had his HGV. His son worked in racing, in a National Hunt yard in Somerset. It turned out that we knew quite a few of the same people. Racing is a small world. Not many people who came to work at Woodside had worked in a jump yard. There is a difference, the jump yards are more how do I say this? Rough and ready? No, that's not it. More down to earth? That could be it, although most of the staff at Woodside were okay.

Bryan knew his stuff. We tended to be put down as a pair of old codgers who knew nothing. So we would stand there and laugh together about how little we knew. Funny how when things went tits up, it was us two, called upon to sort it out a lot of the time. It was also us two, who could see the damage that was being done to horses by the vets who had been drafted in from Newmarket. The original vets we had used for years were pushed out by these new vets. From what we could see, they were not animal lovers. It was all about how much money they could make.

It was Bryan who saved one of the yard men from being trampled. This man had gone in to a colts stable, the colt had taken exception to him, for whatever reason. He floored the man, luckily Bryan was walking past and saw the colt waving his front legs in the air about to come down on the yard man. He got him out just in time.

One of my lasting impressions of Bryan was when we had our Christmas do at Newbury Racecourse. I picked Bryan and his missus up and drove us there, we didn't want to be reliant on the mini bus for getting us home. He got plastered, insisted on sitting on the throne that was there. No idea why that was there, but hey ho! We couldn't get him off that throne when it was time to go. He had helped himself to a bottle of wine off the table, as he was putting his coat on. We had quite a few stairs to go down before we arrived outside. Full marks to him for clutching his bottle of wine, like long lost treasure as he slid down three flights of stairs. Amazingly he stayed upright and more importantly the wine was still in one piece. His missus and myself got him in the back of the Jeep where he promptly passed out. In fact by the time I got in the drivers seat he was snoring away. He would come to occasionally, coming up for air like a dying fish, peer through the windows and pass out again. His missus was not impressed. I left her to it when we arrived at their house. Her man, her job. Amazingly he was fine the next day!

54

CHANGE OF MANAGEMENT

When Bertie retired, the company employed another trainer from a yard in Newmarket. He really did have a steep learning curve ahead of him. He had massive boots to fill. I mean how do you follow a racing dynasty like Bertie? Fair play to Oliver for giving it a go. Our head lad Sam helped him out no end, he was well aware of the enormous task ahead of Oliver. The company wanted Sam to take on the trainers role, but he turned it down. At the time he liked his job as head lad.

Oliver tried to be fair, but as more staff and horses arrived, I think he got slightly out of his depth. Certain staff members, not the original ones I might add, took advantage of him. If I was short staffed on the yards when people were away racing, I would say to him that we needed help on the yards. He would nearly always be behind me rolling his sleeves up, and he would get stuck in to whatever needed doing. Not many trainers, especially in a place like Woodside would have done that.

When I finished my Equine Massage training, I achieved a mark of distinction. I spoke to one of our original vets who I regularly helped in the vet box, if they were happy for me to treat some of the horses on the yard. You have to get permission from the vet because there could be an underlying problem with a certain horse and massage might be detrimental to the horse. She was happy enough for me to go ahead, so I went to see Oliver. I didn't want to remain on the yard forever, I got myself trained in quite a few things and I wanted to progress.

Oliver seemed to be quite happy for me to show him how I would treat a horse, so we picked one of the horses I looked after, so he could make up his own mind. After spending an hour telling him what I had found and why I was treating the horse in a certain way. I had completed my massage, we left the stable. I overheard him say when he was asked how it had gone, that he had just had a lesson in anatomy. Clearly I had talked too much about what I had found, but I thought that was the whole idea. I was wrong. I never heard another word from Oliver about treating his horses, although he did get someone in to massage them. So in one way the horses benefited. This became a trend over the next three years. A couple of good jobs became available, but I wasn't considered, I was stuck on the yard, admittedly well paid and in lovely surroundings. My head lad once said that I was the best yardy he had ever seen. He had worked in racing for many years. Praise indeed. Or maybe a curse.

55

Sam was another incredibly hard working person in racing, there are a hell of a lot of these people, who don't receive the credit they are due. He just doesn't stop. He really does love his horses. He is such a kind man, both to the horses and people. He rarely asked for help, even when it was really needed. He did his back in very badly, he could barely walk, but he was in work, starting at his usual silly o'clock to get the horses fed before exercise. When everyone else went home at lunch, he often carried on working through till evening stables and beyond. He did most of the 10pm checks on the yards. It was nearly always between 6pm and 10pm that a horse would be discovered cast or ill.

He did most of the breaking of the yearlings with his friend Paul. They work together very well as a team. They rode all the yearlings to ensure that the riders would be safe, when the time came to hand the yearlings over to the other riders. They also watched as all their hard work went down the pan with some inconsiderate riders, who thought that they were the dogs bollocks or just plain scared of riding yearlings. He never expected any one to do something that he himself couldn't do. If a horse kicks out unexpectedly, I have seen him put himself between that horse and a member of staff. Not many people do that!

His veterinary knowledge is second to none. In fact, I went to him if I had a problem with my own horse before I called the vet. This also carried on when I got my lurcher who kept going through fences. I learnt a lot from him, just watching how he did things. That to my mind is a sign of a good head lad. He very rarely lost his temper, but when he did, it was best to take cover and hide.

It was down to him, who looked after which horses on the night at evening stables. Before Oliver, the boss turned up, he did the work board, matching his horses with the riders who would get the best results from these horses. As time has gone on, this man who is bloody good at his job, the company think an awful lot of him, has been pushed out and excluded from important decisions by people, who have no idea that if it wasn't for him, there would be no Woodside. They owe him a lot and a bit of respect would go a long way.

When the washing machines break down, it's Sam who takes all the bandages, rubbers and pads home to wash in his own washing machine, so that the horses have clean gear for the next morning. He knows how everything works on the place. Mind you, he has been there long enough.

When he lets his hair down, he really lets his hair down. Christmas parties are a trial for his long suffering wife. One year at the local pub, he decided to stand on a chair to give a speech to say how grateful he was to his staff, he overbalanced and ended up going backwards through the french windows, not once but twice. At Paul's one evening, after a barbecue, he decided that he was going home, he had had enough to drink. No shit Sherlock! When he couldn't find his way out of the house we knew he was in trouble. We offered to walk him home just across the way. But no, he could find his own way home. He was seen crawling on his hands and knees over the sleeping policemen on the drive. He was heading in the right direction, whether his wife would let him in the house or not was another matter!

56

THE SECRETARY

Rodger came to us, after the untimely death of Bertie's son, The horses were sent to other trainers and the yard was dispersed. He was actually quite a good secretary. Admittedly we didn't think so at the time. He was a bit of a stickler for rules and regulations, but he came at the right time. We were getting more and more horses. Sam's wife who had been acting as our secretary was getting a bit snowed under, she had her own full time job in the village. She would spend her evenings doing office work for the company.

I don't know how he wrangled it, but he got a house on the estate. These were for racing staff, technically he was racing staff, but secretaries tend to live away from the yard. He did share the house with one of the stable lasses, who he would often lock inside the house. She would escape by climbing through a downstairs window. I think he had a key fetish. If there was a lock, he would have the key to it and the key would be in his little black box. He did love his little black box.

If there was an emergency on the yard, he would have been of no use whatsoever. Once, there was an emergency, well

Charlie, Bertie's other son who trains horses at the other end of Lambourn did. He had a horse who was colicking badly and their lorry was out of action. The horse had to go to the vets in Newbury. We had a two horse box on the yard and he wouldn't let them use it. They managed to get some transport from another yard and the horse did survive, no thanks to Rodger.

Rodger had all the keys to the vehicles that were owned by the company and parked on the yard in his box. It was one of those savings boxes with a small lock on the front of it. He would walk around with this box attached to his hand like a handbag. We all were convinced that he slept with it. The problem with being so security conscious was that it was a fight to get any of the keys off him. The vehicles batteries were always going flat in winter. If we had needed the lorry in an emergency, it probably wouldn't have started.

To be fair if you did have a problem then he would try to find a solution, he helped me out a few times. A Spanish girl started working for us and she had no where to live, so I foolishly said she could move in with me temporarily. What a dick I am. Her dog damaged the doors and windows in the house. It broke it's way out of a cage that she had used to transport the dog over from Spain by air. Good job it didn't do that whilst, it was in the air. It was borderline insane. She shut MY dogs out when I wasn't at home, damaged my furniture and ran up huge bills, all within two weeks. This was why no one would put her up. Thankfully Rodger arranged for her to be moved on. But he did have a sinister side, he did a number on me with Oliver when I stood up to him one time.

He was very good at following the horses, both ours and those of other trainers. He would often walk round the yards, he took a real interest in how the horses were going. In fact that became a standing joke, he knew more about our horses and their training than Oliver did.

When our horses were running, he actively encourage all of us to go in the office to watch the race. It didn't matter if we were working, we would down tools, make the horses safe and trooped in to the office. Our next secretary didn't like us going in her office, Sam told her we were all going in to watch our horses run. She had a face like a slapped arse every time one of our horses ran, much to our amusement.

Rodger was also on the ball when it came to organising how much holidays we were entitled to, after he left, our holidays were cut down because they didn't fit in with company policy with the stud side of the business. I found out that, when I questioned about the holiday entitlement, I had lost two days, the new secretary had cut days off my holidays. I ended up with twenty six and a half days, when I should have received thirty. I wasn't the only one to be short changed.

When Rodger left, I applied for the job as secretary. I had attended a racing secretary's course at The British Racing School in Newmarket, I had also done office experience in a racing yard with a very good secretary. But computer said 'No'. Although I was offered the chance to go in the office after morning stables to help the new secretary who, from what I had been told had not attended the secretarial course, and I was to do this for free. I'm sure you can imagine my reply.

Whenever anyone went in the office she was always on Facebook, more than once I had to stand over her, to make sure that the orders for the hay or shavings that we needed, were ordered, it had been forgotten about more than once. In fact the only time she was properly civil to the staff was when there were other people in the office or Oliver was in, and had his door open.

The company did most of the secretarial work from Newmarket. They paid us, but we noticed that the £10 bonus we received, when the horse we looked after won, was stopped after Rodger left. Thank god they paid us and not the new secretary, as only the favourites would get any wages! When the favourites ran out of holiday leave, it didn't matter as they were still able to take paid days off. It was unbelievable. But, the company were very good to me when I became very ill.

The new secretary was on the ball, when I was having a problem with someone who used to live with me on the estate. They had moved out of the house, but for whatever reason would go back to the house whilst I was at work. As soon as I told the secretary what I suspected was happening, she got the locks changed on the house. End of problem and thank you very much.

57

THE ASSISTANT

Our pupil assistant Ross, started out really well. Nothing was too much trouble. He really wanted to prove himself. He encouraged staff to go to him if they had an issue, this made a refreshing change from the previous year after Bertie had left. He worked damned hard. Then it all started to go downhill. He had some really good ideas and he was knowledgable, I learnt new things from him. But we got the impression that he had become disillusioned. Then other staff members were employed and he definitely went downhill.

Ross would find fault with the staff who actually did their work, and turn a blind eye to ones that didn't. He would get someone to cover up their tardiness, like wheelbarrows being left full, in the middle of the yard when there had been plenty of time to empty them. The excuse was always that the groundsmen hadn't emptied the trailers on time. This was mostly rot, as it was the first job they did before going on to their other jobs. I had a blazing row with him one morning, I had been helping one of the farriers with a horse and had just sat down on a wheelbarrow, when the assistant appeared. The first thing he did was have a go about me sitting on the barrow and told me to empty his pals barrow that had been dumped in the middle of the yard, yet again. At first I said no, then I emptied it to keep the peace, but he went on, and so did I. I started to walk out of the yard as I had enough of him by this stage, and he was shouting 'are you walking out Billie?'

'No, I want you to sack me'. It didn't happen, I had to skulk back in to the yard. That was another occasion that I bent Bryan's ear lol.

I just didn't understand why Ross stayed, he was good at his job, but was failing good and proper. Being management level he shouldn't have been as friendly with some of the staff as he was. Outside of work, yes. But inside, no. New girls who arrived on the yard were added to his harem. He started to bring his vape thing on the yard. It was nothing to see him striding about with smoke coming from his trousers. Maybe he thought he looked cool, but it was a standing joke that he looked like he was sucking on a sex toy!

With all the crap that was starting to go on, my opinion of him went west good and proper when, he decided to take all the horses temperatures. About time I thought. The only time these horses had their temperatures taken was if they were off colour or the vet took it. Ross started off in the top two yards, he never once cleaned the thermometer, he made his way round to the two bottom yards, again not cleaning the thermometer. Seriously, how hard is it to have basic cleanliness? We had a hundred horses in training, anyone of them could have had a virus.

Then there was the time both the yard men down the bottom yards were off sick. To be fair Ross rolled his sleeves up and got stuck in. Neither of us realised just how bad those forty stables were. But what can you expect when these two guys were working their backsides off, and not getting any help from the yard men from the top yards who, were only mucking out eight horses apiece and refused to muck out any more.

We had to gut near enough all forty stables, Ross was nearly in tears, personally, I wanted to fillet the two foreign guys in the top yards.

Ross was very clicky with the secretary, they hatched a plan to see what the staff who lived on site had in their houses. We had had no house checks for years, and these two gave us very little warning that they were coming round. Personally I didn't have a problem with them wanting to check the house as I had a couple of issues that I hoped would be fixed. I did however have a bit of a problem when the assistant informed me that he was moving a new member of staff in to my house with me. He had done this a couple of times before and I had said no, that was my home. This time he basically said that if I didn't accept the girl, then I had to move out of the house. Which would have been fine had I been offered one of the companies smaller houses. Non of the other staff members living in a house on site were treated like this. So I locked horns with him, again. I didn't want to be a grass, but with hindsight I should have gone to head office, as the behaviour of the management there at the time was dragging the company down.

When we all moved in to these houses there was nothing in them at all. Not even a cooker. We furnished these houses ourselves and there is nothing wrong with that. The company did eventually put a brand new kitchen in to a couple of houses. My house had one and it was very nice, although the man who put it in, tried to make off with my cooker. I was expected to provide all the furnishings, plates, cutlery, pans, washing machine, dryer, you name it, for the new members of staff that management were putting in to my home. My daughter had moved out by this time. The head office had no idea that this was going on and were horrified when they did find out. Turned out the girl was nice, she was no problem at all. We split the bills for the electric and the oil that we ordered, down the middle. But that was not the point.

When I finally left Woodside, Oliver sent his secretary round with £100 to cover the cost of the oil that I had paid for. I got someone to measure the contents of the tank, and I was out of pocket by £300. I went to head office directly and they paid me the remainder straight away, I should have gone to them in the first place. They would have offered me a smaller house, which I would have been happy with. The house I was in, was for a family. But I got the distinct impression from the management on the yard, that the houses were for the riders and no one else. But I was done by this time.

58

TRANSPORTING HORSES

The company were generous when it came to looking after it's staff and horses. We were very well looked after. The horses wanted for nothing, well apart from a decent vet by this time, but you can't have everything. We had a small two horse box that was getting on a bit, so that was replaced and then a year or so later they bought a four horse lorry that required an HGV driver. We had been relying on local horse transport to take our horses racing or to the vets. We had big horses, our problem could be that the small box would be overweight and not big enough. When our horses went back to the stud, were brought back to us to resume training, or were picked up from Stanstead after wintering in Dubai, the company's own lorries did the transporting. But, when the horses went racing, transport companies were used. One of the companies we used had a driver, who as soon as they arrived at Woodside, would hotfoot it to the toilet in the medical room. They would spend ages in there and bung the toilet up as well. We wondered if they actually had a toilet of their own.

There were three of us with our HGV licences. Bryan, myself

and a new employee who was busily entrenching himself up the managements backside. Yes, you guessed it Bryan and myself stood no chance despite having plenty of experience of driving lorries, and more importantly driving a lorry with a horse on board. The new guy got the job, fair play to him if he could drive the lorry. He had some experience driving, but he didn't have a clue when it came to driving this kind of lorry. He went to pick up the brand new lorry, on the way back from the outfitters he hit a bus in the lanes. We couldn't believe it was in pieces already. He came in for a serious amount of mickey taking from the lads, instead of taking it on the chin like most people would, he got real shirty. It was pointed out to him numerous times that if it had happened to anyone else, he would be first in line to criticise and it would have been relentless too.

A week later, he was driving the lorry back to Swindon to get it repaired and it broke down. When the lorry finally arrived back on the yard in one piece and working, our new lad was let out on the road with a horse on board. I'll leave that there....

The ramp for loading the horses was opposite the two bottom yards that housed the yearlings. Bryan and myself were working there and noticed that the lorry wasn't left running when it was going somewhere, it needed about twenty minutes running time to warm the engine up before you could go anywhere in it. After a few runs, we said something to the management as it would be no fun to break down on the motorway with a horse on board. But in all honesty we shouldn't have had to say anything.

I didn't understand why the travelling head lass was not considered to be put forward to take her HGV. In most race yards, the travelling lads did most of the driving to move the horses around. But I was becoming to realise that I had absolutely no idea whatsoever, why a lot of things were done there. It had come down to, if your face fitted, not how experienced and how well people did their job.

As Woodside was a biggish yard, we had two travelling people. Every year they clashed. Every year, sides were taken by the other members of staff. Some would swear that they would not go racing with so and so. Then the following week they were put on the lorry with their horse, with the one they didn't want to go racing with, and behave as though they hadn't said anything mean about that travelling person. That used to make me laugh..

The travelling head lass, kept the racing tack in good nick and put in the order for new tack when the need arose. Unfortunately, she had a habit of taking all the good stuff with her when she went racing and leaving the not so good racing tack for the second travelling person. This caused no end of rows. The second travelling was Paul and he was fairly docile until his racing tack went walkabout. Half the problem was who owned the yard and the horses. Our horses were expected to be turned out immaculately. Our horses just couldn't run in any old tack. The competition each season was all about who brought home the most winners. It was more like a soap opera than a race yard. Quite entertaining when you weren't in the middle of it.

59

MONDAY MORNINGS

Monday mornings in racing can often be approached with trepidation. This was especially true in our yard. As I said before, Phil had barely any horse knowledge, in most race yards the horses feed is cut down over the weekend. The majority are not going to be ridden till Monday morning so they don't need packing full of rocket fuel. Our poor riders on Mondays, I'm surprised that they turned up for work.

It doesn't do the horses any good to be fed their training mix on the weekend. Quite a few of them got Azoturia, which is when a horses muscles cramp mainly in the hind end because they have been fed too much rich feed and haven't had the exercise to work it off. The muscles are full of lactic acid and if left untreated this can damage the muscles.

At first Bryan and myself wore our safety work boots that were issued to us, but in time particularly Monday mornings, we wore trainers, as we could run better in them. Well Bryan could, I'm permanently lame, so my running left a lot to be desired. After legging the riders up, we would rush to get as much done as possible before the riders started to fall off. A good morning was when no one fell off before they got to the gallop. The gates to the gallop were shut behind them in an attempt to keep the loose horses in one place. It wasn't the riders fault, it was because the horses were not fed correctly for the work that they were doing. This was down to management not passing information on to Phil in the feed room.

When our phones started ringing to say, that a loose one was heading our way or that we were to get on the gallop and catch a loose horse, we were hopefully ready. With the gates to the gallop shut it wasn't so bad. The horse was contained, sort of! I would check that all the gates were shut to the gallop. Some of the riders would be at the top circling round, nearly all of them were on their phones and had no idea what was happening around them.

I would get 'what are you doing here?'

'I'm here to catch the loose horse!'

Then it was 'oh, who's come off?' Absolutely no clue.

I would then say rather sarcastically, 'well the slap as the rider hit the ground and the horse buggering off is usually a clue'. Even when a rider was in hot pursuit of their horse, after they had done an unplanned dismount, wasn't noticed some of the time. Sometimes the horse would make it's way back to the gates, all you would hear was the hoof beats as the horse appeared out of the mist. Facebook and Instagram have a lot to answer for!

The office is a small square building, standing by it's self. When I first started work at Woodside there was a hedge running all around it. Someone decided that they didn't want the hedge there, so it was pulled out. Great. For some reason the loose horses if they got as far as the office would run round the hedge, they would just follow it round. When the hedge was gone they made a beeline to those damn electric gates. The very gates that first thing in the morning wouldn't open to let me out, to do my own horse. They would miraculously open when a riderless horse was heading down the drive. I would be running, well in my case hobbling after the horse saying under my breath, 'please let the gates stay shut'. I was pushing the boundaries of athleticism and failing on a daily basis.

Too many people had the phone code for the gate, the staff should have it, but other people shouldn't have access to it. They would turn in to Woodside off the main road, phone the code as soon as they were on the drive, and the gates would open like sesame at our end. It is a long drive, why they couldn't wait till they got to the gates was beyond me. Sooner or later a horse will go through those gates and on to the road and it won't be pretty.

Monday mornings were our main days for being kicked, bit or shagged, as we rounded up the loose horses and put the riders back on board. Our lives would flash before our eyes at times. Especially when we had to get in between two horses squaring up to each other. It was usually colts with all those hormones raging!

60

THE HORSES

We had beautiful horses at Woodside, thoroughbreds are beautiful anyway, well I think so, but then I am biased. The horses at Woodside were exceptional, they were very well bred horses, in class of their own. Some of these horses stayed a while and some didn't. A lot depends on how well they run, how they coped with the training itself, and, you may find this surprising, how well the company likes that particular horse. We had horses who were pretty much useless for racing but were spared from being sent to the sales as the company liked them, a job would be found for them, usually leading the babies. The company had horses in training all over the place with different trainers, as they owned Woodside, we would get all sorts of company horses with problems coming to us.

We got quite a few stale horses, our head lads job, would be to freshen then up, if he could. Hopefully the horse hadn't gone too far down the road to being sour. Sam usually succeeded, but there a couple of horses that arrived from France, one was a complete pig, there was no other word to describe him. Our French guy wanted him, I think it was the French thing! I was stuck with the horse, so I jumped at the chance to get shot of him. I swapped him for a little filly who our French guy looked after. I like fillies. Within two weeks our French guy wasn't that pleased with the horse. It also dumped one of our jockeys who had come in on a work day to put it through it's paces. The horse then proceeded to run amok through two lots of sheep wire and some barbed wire. When it came back on the yard there was barely a mark on it. Anything else would have been ripped to bits. This horse came with a lovely looking grey, which looked more like a showjumper than a racehorse. He was a nice person, but hated racing. He wouldn't start in his races. Everything was tried, he went for jollies to Kempton and Lingfield. It was a waste of time. Eventually, after trying just about everything to get the horse to start, the company sent him to the sales and an Irish yard bought him as a hurdler. He did start for them as there were no stalls to go in, he won a race, but it was a bit hit or miss if he would start. He was quite famous for it. I heard recently that he had died. He was a lovely horse, but not a racehorse.

There was quite a bit of excitement when the first Frankel arrived on the yard. He arrived with another horse that cost a fraction of what the Frankel had cost. In fact the cheap horse was the better horse, he looked better, his conformation was better, but he turned out to have two sticky stifle joints. The expensive horse looked weak and we were right, he was a tall horse. He broke the first day he was ridden. He had to go back to the stud, mainly to strengthen up. He came back to Woodside a year later and promptly broke again. Some horses are just not meant to be racehorses. It doesn't matter how well they are bred, if it's not meant to be then that's basically it. Game over.

We had quite few horses by Dubawi. There is a certain look

to a lot of horses, you can sometimes pick up their sire just by looking at the horse. The sire and the dams can throw certain attributes to their offspring, it could be their mannerisms, the way they move, it could be certain points of their head. Dubawi's tend to have chunky heads with large cheek bones. When I was at Barber's, RB liked Mister Lord horses. Most of them had large ears, goat like eyes and flat feet, but RB was successful with them. Most trainers have a favourite stallion that they like their horses to come from. One of the most prolific sires is Galileo, a lot of racehorses nowadays go back to him and that bloodline.

61

THE COMPANY

We had a number of successful horses, but we could have had a whole lot more. The breeding was there. For whatever reason, a heck of a lot of the horses would go wrong and in one season alone, an awful lot were sent back to the stud to mend and recuperate. We were exceptionally lucky to have this option, most trainers do not. But then we only had the one owner, we had a couple of horses each year that belonged to a friend of his. He had some cracking horses in training with us.

Some of the horses we would get each year had wintered in Dubai. They were something else. They looked more like store cattle than racehorses. They were big, big two year olds. Considering the distance they had travelled they were remarkably sane. The odd one lost the plot along the way, but they were very few. One huge chestnut colt liked to stand in his manger and try to shag the wall. Needless to say, he broke his manger. It had to be seen to be believed. These horses were so well treated from the time they were born in the studs. They genuinely liked us humans. They really did have the best of everything. If they were lying down in their stables when you went in, there was no frantic getting to their feet because they felt vulnerable, they had nothing to fear from us. Hopefully, it would remain like that throughout their lives.

It was an eye opener working for this company. Everything is done on a different scale. The amount of horses that they buy at the sales, which ones are sold, which fillies they decide to breed from, which colts they decide to geld. I wouldn't have missed this for the world. I learnt such a lot.

On the days when the racing manager would come down from Newmarket to discuss how each and every horse is progressing, I learnt how differently he looked at the horses, each horse was looked at as an individual, they went out of their way to provide the best healthcare and how might the training be adjusted to suit that particular horse. At the end of the day they want the best results from their horses, they are not afraid to chuck money at them to get the results they want.

When the owner came to see his horses, that was an event. All the windows would be cleaned, the walls in the yard were scrubbed, as were the doors to all the stables. Luckily we had a yard hoover which had the yards pristine in very little time. Our Frenchman loved the hoover! We didn't always know if he was coming by helicopter or road until about an hour before he arrived. Sometimes he would arrive early and we would bump in to him and his entourage, as we were running from yard to yard tidying up. Every single horse would be pulled out of their stable, one at a time and shown to him. Sam was very good at giving the talk about each horse, Oliver not so. Whereas Sam would be relaxed, Oliver would be hyperventilating. His lack of knowledge would be found out.

In my last year at Woodside, our owner visited more than he

normally did. It wasn't to see all of his horses, it was just to see a couple at a time. This in itself was unusual, one of the last visits I was there for, was on a Sunday. It was an epic foul up from start to finish. We were down the bottom yards, as that was where the horses he wanted to see were stabled. To begin with the gates were locked, the lad on the gate didn't recognise the car, he had come in a different one than usual. When he was recognised and let through, he drove on down to us. Parked at the top of the yard. He got out, stone me, he looked ticked off. Oliver got the lads to pull the horses out for him to look at. It went downhill rapidly from then on. Our owners son was also in the car, he must have thought that he would lighten the mood. He skipped from the car, and stood behind his father waving at us lot standing against the stables, we went to wave back. Then our owners head turned slowly towards us. We could feel the laser beams of rage coming out from behind the dark glasses and we decided not to wave. Best not in the circumstances. Clearly he was not having a good day.

Most of the time when our owner came, he was very generous and showed his appreciation for our hard work by leaving everyone a little brown envelope. The horses had the best shavings on the market, there was none of the only two bales a week nonsense that most stables used. The horses are living in a stable twenty three hours a day and hopefully, earning the yard some money, so they were bedded up properly, to make them comfortable. We were allowed to use as many bales of shavings as needed. Bliss!

We had North American green hay imported in, we had two different types of small bale hay, there was haylage. There were at least two different types of shavings, sometimes we had three or four different types of shavings. Yearlings are mucky buggers so we would use cheaper shavings on them. Each year we would have brand new rugs, the best ones would go on the horses that wouldn't trash them. There was brand new tack regularly bought from the local tack shop. The riders were kitted out with brand new hats and body protectors. The local tack shop loved us. The hay company, not so. If the hay was inferior then it was sent back; the whole lot. We had over a hundred bales a week coming in. The men who delivered the hay certainly worked for their money, each bale was manually put on and off the lorries. Christmas and New Year was a logistical nightmare. We had to make sure we had enough of everything to cover us for the minimum of two weeks. Fortunately our barn was large, but even so the shavings were often left on their pallets outside so that we could get the hay and other feedstuff inside the barn. The hay company closed down for the whole Christmas and New Year period. Thankfully we had the machinery at our end to transport the pallets around ourselves. The company made sure we had everything that was needed. It certainly made our job on the ground a lot easier.

The company was on the ball when it came to health and safety. When the men came down from head office to conduct the resuscitation course, they arrived with models of babies! There wasn't a baby anywhere near the place, well some of the staff members were a bit soft, but really? What were we supposed to do with that? We handled horses all day everyday. What I did learn was that if we did have a fire, when we got the horses out, we were to shut the doors to their stables as they could return to their stable, they felt safe in there.

62

MARKAZ

Our first Dark Angel colt arrived with another four horses from our stud in Ireland. He behaved like an absolute brat and I loved him! I don't normally go for greys and I usually like fillies, but Markaz was special. Admittedly a bit special needs at times, he had plenty of character and he was a kind horse, when he wasn't behaving like a dick. He tried the patience of his riders on a regular basis. One of his tricks was to go in to the ride, stand up on his back legs and wave to everyone. He got his feet stuck on the top rail one morning, his front shoes got caught on the ledge that ran round the indoor ride. He was always a gentleman with me.

He raced in Baden Baden in Germany, Paul and one of the other lads took him. Instead of flying him there the decision was taken to drive, in the hopes that the horse would be more manageable at the other end, plus it was cheaper! He ran a good race but was placed second after a photo finish. We were robbed, I tell you.

When he arrived back in Lambourn, Sam, my head lad told me Markaz was out in one of the paddocks, a rare treat for him. When I went to get him, I called his name and he came cantering over to me straight away. That said it all for me. He was pleased to see his mum! Colts don't normally give a damn about most things as long as they are fed, watered, warm and comfortable.

I looked after him for the duration of his time at Woodside until he retired to stand at Derrinstown Stud in Ireland. I'll never forget looking at the huge lorry that had come over for him. He was going to be travelling in style, but I was more concerned with him travelling alone for hours and the fact that when the ferry sets sail, no one is allowed in the hold until the ship docks. Anything could happen. The ship could sink, he could have got colic, he could have wrapped his front legs round something, I know I'm being a bit melodramatic, but this was Markaz we were talking about!! I cried the tears of the grieving widow. I have never cried over any other horse in racing. There are those who I still think about, even now, wondering if they are being properly cared for, but I never cried over them. I felt sad when they left, but there were always so many other horses to look after and ride.

Oliver very kindly gave me both of Markaz's silver plated plates from when he won The Chip Chase Stakes at Newcastle. I kept in touch with the stud for a while. Their secretary was happy to keep me posted on how Markaz was settling in to his new life. I received updates about his first teaser mare and his first covering. He was a gentleman I'm happy to say. I was a proud mummy again! On the studs website he looks a million dollars, he has faded in colour from the iron grey he was when he was racing, to a light dapple grey, he looks so happy and handsome, of course! Good result.

63

WINTER WONDERLAND

Woodside is a beautiful place in all seasons, in winter when the frost comes, the trees are covered in snow, it becomes a magical winter wonderland. It's freezing cold, well, it is situated on top of a hill.

Most of the stables are kitted out with heat lamps which go on when the weather is seriously cold. Most of the taps have heaters on them to stop them from freezing. Like I said, the company thinks of most things and provides them. You still had to insulate the taps with feed sacks on really cold nights. This was something the head lad on one of the yards, on my weekend on failed to grasp. The temperature sunk to -10 overnight and told he us not to bother insulating the taps. Some of us ignored him and wrapped bags around some of the taps, just as well we did. Of course everything froze. We had very little water for the horses, thankfully, one of the grounds men brought a trailer round which had sides that went down. We filled containers of every dimension, put them on the trailer and he took this round the yards. We had limited water for a few days because of that particular head lad, not the main head lad I hasten to add.

Luckily the taps started to thaw with plenty of hot water, so we managed to get all the taps working in each yard.

We also had the most snow fall on my weekends on. Joy! After doing the horses, instead of going home, we would get stuck in to clearing the walkways and the yards for the following morning. The amount of salt we went through was immense. I have a lasting image of one of our yard lads who had never seen snow before, just walking through the stuff in amazement. He loved the snow. He didn't care when he got cold, it was all so new to him.

Most of us had dogs, we would often walk them all together after work. We could walk them anywhere we wanted on the estate. In the field at the back of our houses, the snow was really deep and my terrier would sink up past his back. My lurcher had the best time running round, she hadn't had the best start to life. I didn't get her till she was three, she had been shut in a stable all that time, so to see her run round with the other dogs was lovely. She learnt to play at Woodside and be a proper dog at last. Admittedly I kept losing her at first, but she always came back.

Being on top of a hill could have it's drawbacks, being colder was one. Having Chinook helicopters flying very close to the roofs of our houses was another. We had to make sure that we had enough oil for heating. We were a good mile from the village, so again we had to have enough provisions for when it did snow, as it could be difficult to get to the shops. You really didn't want to risk walking down to the village in snow, there was black ice and stupid drivers to contend with. I saw more upturned cars in and around Lambourn than anywhere else I have lived, mostly due to the black ice on the roads and people driving too fast.

Coming home from evening stables one night before I worked at Woodside. I came round a bend, there in front of me was a young girl trying to crawl out of her car that had gone in a ditch. I stopped, put my hazards on, praying that no one would hit my car and got out, I couldn't stand up! I was on sheet ice. Another car coming from the other way managed to stop and between us we got the girl to safety. If a car had hit either one of our cars we would have been in serious shit, as there was no traction whatsoever. The girl was alright, badly shaken up, her car was a right off, but she was safe.

Leaving the house early to do my horse, I loved walking and driving on crisp, dry, virgin snow. Although it was hazardous when it was icy. The council were good at salting the roads, but there wasn't a lot you could do when the weight of the snow brought trees down. I often came across cars that were abandoned after they had skidded and hit trees, banks or walls. Thankfully no one was in them.

All in all, it was a beautiful place to live and work in. You just had to be prepared for the changes in the weather and the fact that we were out in the sticks, we helped each other out.

In the summer the weather could be absolutely baking hot one minute and cold the next. I have photos of summer days with the sun shining and then an hour later it was hailing. The weather could be weird in Lambourn. When the weather was very hot, we would start work an hour earlier, in the hope that we would have finished exercising the horses before it got too hot. Then we would be roasted alive doing evening stables.

64

THIEVES

As it drew near to Christmas each year we had a visit from thieves, they were as regular as clockwork. They would come in the back way. There is a track running between the main road that takes you into the next village at one end, and Farncombe which at is the other end and where our grass gallops were. We had a gate on the side of the track, which led to the all weather gallop. The thieves would drive up the track, go through wooden gate, literally, they weren't fussy. Then drive across the gallop and the field to get to where the sheds were that housed our equipment. There were all sorts of power tools that they wanted, so they took them. Eventually, the tractors were put across the doors so that no one could get in the sheds, but that took a few years for that to sink in. Instead of replacing the wooden gates each year, they now have metal gates.

The tack room in the main yard was emptied one time. When the police arrived they paid a visit to the stud next door to see if they had been targeted as well. The police had had no report from them, but it was still early in the morning. When they arrived there, the tack was found hidden behind their Discovery.

Very strange! But at least we got everything back that time.

In time more gates were put on the estate to protect it from thieves. It was too open, in the winter months we did see more 4X4's and vans driving round the back of the place. The farm behind us was locked up tighter than a bank vault, they were hit most years as well. The farrier supply store which was across the road from the farm next door, was rammed and their stuff taken. They fought back by sinking railway sleepers in to the ground, if anything tried to go over that, their vehicles would be ruined.

65

RACING PEOPLE

Racing people are definitely different to other people. We look at things in a different way. When things go wrong we are more likely to shrug our shoulders and go 'oh well'. We tend to be stoic about things. We have to be. We are out in all weathers, work all hours. Stable staff are well looked after today, compared with the stable staff of years ago. Yes it can be a dangerous job, but it is the best job in the world. I have worked in most jobs in the equine industry, and I have to say hand on heart, that racing for me, was and is the best.

Not many jobs give their employees the opportunity to travel the world, some travel with their horses to races in Dubai, USA, Japan, Australia and other places. Other people choose to go and work in these places for an indefinite time, leaving all that is familiar many miles behind them. In all these scenarios you are constantly learning. Each job teaches you new things, some good, some bad. Some jobs leave you with a nasty taste in your mouth and have you questioning yourself. Are you in the right job? Are you cut out to work with horses? It can also show you how not to do things. It is certainly character building. Each horse you handle, teaches you something new.

The kids coming in to racing these days seem to be mostly told, that they are good enough to be a jockey. They are told this at Racing School when they start their apprenticeship. They can't even sweep a yard properly, without complaining that it is beneath them. In most cases they do not ride well enough for a trainer to take a chance on them, in order for them to become the yards apprentice. It takes work, practice and riding the crappy horses, that just love to dump their riders at the first opportunity. It's the tricky horses that teach you your job. You don't learn sitting pretty in the perfect position on a horse that does nothing wrong.

One of the best riders I have seen in recent years on the last yard I worked at, was sidelined quite a bit, because he would go and help his father who was also a trainer. The bosses didn't seem to get, that they needed this lad sat on a horse, not mucking out. If he had been treated better, he might not have kept disappearing to help his dad. He could ride anything and ride it well.

Racing is a harsh industry. I've known head lads who think that is quite okay to hit a horse round it's back end with the buckles of a girth, and try to chase a nervous filly out of her stable when she was frightened of hitting her head.

I've seen a trainer put an injured horse on a walker fully tacked up with her head tied down, because an hour earlier, the horse had flipped over when the trainer went to get on her. The mare had a fractured cheek and nose, blood was pouring out of her nose and I made her take that horse off the walker. I threatened to report her to the British Horse Racing Authority if the mare did not receive medical attention. The mare didn't see the vet and I did report her. The representatives of this organisation were spotted going in to the yard, but were headed off in another direction by a trainer of a small string of Arabs, who also trained out of this yard. They were more interested in training their small string of Arabs than the welfare of a badly injured horse. A year later the horse was sold to a local man up the road for him to ride in Point to Points, it bolted with him, not just once, it nearly killed him. He got the horse properly checked out and she was found to have kissing spine. She was in agony when being ridden. She wasn't a cheap buy either.

Then there was the trainer who sent a horse racing that had no right to be on the racetrack, it's legs were so bad it only made it once round the track before it broke down so badly that it ended up being put down at home. The horse suffered a long journey back to his stables, arriving late at night, his stable wasn't done up, no clean water, hay, nothing. The bag of drugs that the vets at the race course supplied for the horse, were taken off the groom and thrown in a corner and forgotten about. Absolutely disgusting behaviour. Fortunately it doesn't happen often. The fact that it did happen is bad enough. There is no excuse. These trainers let the whole industry down.

Despite these occurrences, there is real kindness within the industry, a lot of the owners will do their upmost to find a horse a good home after it's racing career has ended. There are quite a few rehabilitation places for horses retiring. They do their best to match horses with prospective owners, these horses owe us nothing, but we owe them a lot.

The kindness isn't only for the horses, but for the staff as well. I knew someone who was seriously ill and his boss found out. His boss made him an appointment with a specialist in Harley Street and paid all the bills as well.

There are the just plain daft people who you get everywhere, you stand there shaking your head, wondering 'why?' We had the water cut off for a morning at Woodside, it was all under control with every bucket and most of the wheelbarrows filling up with water. We had enough water for a small siege. Until, Ted appeared to 'help'. Everything he filled up leaked like a sieve, you could see the holes a mile off. Ah well, such is life.

The love lives of the racing fraternity. Well that is something else. If they shag each other, they then hate each other. The ideal if there is an ideal, is to not get involved with someone you work with. Choose someone from another yard. The fallout when it all goes to pot can be immense. The yard is often split down the middle whilst defending some ones honour. The horse walker comes in quite handy for cooling certain people off. One girl wouldn't give her boyfriend any peace, so he put her on the walker, shut the door and turned the electric on. He left her on there for a couple of hours, trotting round. It never occurred to her to lie down and let the partitions go over the top of her.

On the day I left Woodside and racing for good, I drove down that drive for the very last time. I didn't look back. I was so tired. The dogs were in the back of the Jeep. Smartie my old mare, who has been dragged round the country with me over the years, was loaded on the lorry and for once travelled like a dream. Unheard of for her!

The job and lifestyle I had loved for so many years had changed. The job as it was, there at Woodside was not what I went in to racing for. I'll always love my horses and have some brilliant memories. I often think about how the horses that I rode and cared for are doing. I hope that they are well and loved, wherever they may be in the world.

We are going home, at last. Onwards with the next chapter of life........

Acknowledgements

I would like to thank the following people for their help and guidance in writing this book.

Diannah Lowry for egging me on.

Dave Kingdon.

Katie Stephens for her advice when I got stuck on certain issues.

Tamsin Karn for being kind enough to look at photos to help decide which one to use.

And last but not least Julie Humphryes, Emily Mae Stewart, Chris and Jill Leaver and Lynn Uglow for taking the time to read extracts and give me their feed back, good and bad.

Oh! And not forgetting my horsey employers, I learnt from every single one of you. Not always in a good way, but it made me a better person and horsewoman. So thank you.

Printed in Great Britain
by Amazon

24294673R00119